TWO COWBOYS IN NEW YORK

CLARK SELBY

Library of Congress Control Number: 2025913675

ISBN
979-8-89641-079-9 (Paperback)
979-8-89641-080-5 (eBook)
979-8-89641-078-2 (Hardcover)

TABLE OF CONTENTS

1

GOING TO THE WEDDING IN NEW YORK

Indian Leader and his wife, Serene, made plans to travel from the Star Ranch located near Cuero, Texas, to New York City for their friends', Robert Smiley and Joan Sterling, wedding.

Robert had been Indian's best friend since they went to school together on the Cherokee Indian Reservation near Tahlequah, Oklahoma.

This was quite a contrast to where Serene and Joan became best friends; they met at Vassar College in Poughkeepsie, New York, and along with a third friend, Latesha Kay Hudson, they all lived together for four years.

Serene was certain Joan would ask Latesha to be one of her bridesmaids, so the three of them would have the opportunity to spend some time together before the wedding.

It had been years since all three of them had been together, and Serene was certainly looking forward to visiting with both of them again. It would be like old times.

Indian had been in contact with Robert's parents, and they would meet them in Kansas City, and then they would travel together on to New York City. Robert's father, Tom, was from New York and met Robert's mother, a Cherokee princess, White Dove, when they were both studying to be teachers in New York. Because White Dove's father was the chief of the Cherokee and he didn't know about her marriage

1

until she and her new husband came back to the reservation, he told her she was no longer his daughter since she married a white man and without his permission. She would have to leave the reservation.

However, her grandfather, Sequoia, who developed the Cherokee alphabet, spoke up for her; and she was allowed to stay as long as her husband agreed to become a teacher on the reservation. He agreed, and then he was made a member of the tribe.

Robert's mother was also a teacher on the reservation. Indian and Robert had both of Robert's parents for teachers while going to school there.

Before they left the ranch, Indian and Serene had a meeting with the ranch foreman, Lloyd Johnson, to go over several things, to be sure he felt comfortable enough to run the ranch while they were away. Serene told him she had made arrangements for him to be able to draw funds from the Bank of Cuero for the payroll and for the supplies he would need while they were away. Indian told him they were not sure how long they would be gone but probably for at least two or three months. Serene had written information as to how Lloyd could get in contact with them by telegraph if he needed to after they reached New York. Both of them told Lloyd they were sure he could take care of everything at the ranch without any more trouble than he normally had when they were at the ranch.

This would be Indian and Serene's first trip away from the ranch since they had taken three thousand head of longhorns to Dodge City.

They returned from that trip a lot different than when they left with the cattle after Serene had lost her father, who was killed by rustlers. Serene had inherited the ranch upon her father's death. Before her father was killed, he had hired Indian as the trail boss to take the cattle to market. Indian was hired after her father's ranch had lost two herds going to market earlier in the year led by different trail bosses.

Because her father had mortgaged the ranch to buy additional acres to add to the ranch and the loan was due in February, he didn't have enough money to pay off the loan since he hadn't been able to sell the two herds of cattle that were lost on the way to market. Now, he was in danger of losing the ranch if he couldn't get a herd to Dodge City in time to sell it and pay off his loan.

He had spent almost fifty years building the ranch for his daughter, so he had to get some of his cattle to market. With her father's death, Serene had to get the cattle to market to pay off that loan. She certainly didn't intend to lose everything her father had spent years building for her. Her father hired Indian Leader as his trail boss because he had the reputation as being the best trail boss in Texas. He had never lost a man or a herd on a trail drive.

One thing Serene hadn't figured on was falling in love with the trail boss, but she did, and after much hesitation, she agreed to marry him when they reached Dodge City.

Sometimes your best-laid plans don't work out, and this was one of those times. A few days before they arrived in Dodge City, she was kidnapped by men who worked for her neighbor, Kent Eagle. He didn't want her to be able to pay off her dad's loan so he could buy her ranch at a cheap price. The men who kidnapped her took her to Kansas City and held her there to be sure she couldn't pay the loan off even if her cattle got to market in Dodge City. However, Indian got the cattle to market; sold them; made his way back to Cuero, Texas; and paid off the loan. So now her ranch was safe, but she was still kidnapped, and she had no idea Indian sold the cattle and paid off her loan.

Indian's friend, Robert Smiley, whom he met on the trail drive to Dodge City, was able to track the kidnappers and trace Serene all the way to Kansas City. Indian had learned some information in Cuero that helped Robert free Serene; and Indian joined them and her friend, Joan Sterling, in Kansas City. This was where and how Robert and Joan met, and now they were getting married in New York City.

Indian and Serene were married in Kansas City, instead of Dodge City, and they had their two best friends stand up with them at their wedding. Now, they were heading to New York City for their best friends' wedding. Indian and Serene would travel to San Antonio to take a train to Kansas City, where they would meet Robert's parents coming up from Indian Territory.

They took the buggy and the team of horses to San Antonio they had bought in Baxter Springs, Kansas, when they had been coming back to Cuero after getting married in Kansas City. Indian made arrangements to leave their buggy and horses with a livery stable near the railroad station until they returned.

They stayed overnight in a hotel near the train station, so it would be easy to get to their train scheduled to leave at six the next morning. They checked their large trunk in at the depot before they dropped off the buggy at the livery stable, so they only had one small valise to carry to the station with them in the morning.

Six a.m. came as early in San Antonio as it did on the ranch, but they were up at four-thirty, after getting very little sleep, so it wasn't a problem for them. By a little after five, they were at the station, waiting for their train, which would take them all the way to Chicago; and since San Antonio was at the end of the rail line, their train had been waiting for them since sometime last night.

Before boarding the train, Indian checked to be sure their trunk was loaded into one of the baggage cars and that it was checked all the way to New York City. They boarded the train, and the conductor showed them to their Pullman compartment. It was going to be a nicer train ride than the last one Serene had when she was being taken to Kansas City. Her kidnappers told the conductor that she was their sister and their folks asked them to take her to a doctor in Kansas City because she was sick in the head. The kidnappers said she kept telling people she was kidnapped and told her own folks she wasn't their daughter. They said she would tell people she owned a big ranch in Texas instead of living with her folks on a little farm in Kansas. They said sometimes she acted all right, but you never knew what she was going to say or do next.

This time, Serene was traveling with her husband on her way to be in her best friend's wedding and riding in a Pullman compartment on a train that even had a dining car right next to their sleeper car. The trip to Kansas City would take them through Texas, Oklahoma Territory, Kansas, and then into Kansas City, Missouri.

Robert's parents, Tom and White Dove Smiley, were coming by train from Muskogee, Oklahoma Territory, to Kansas City and would meet them; and then they would have a compartment next to them for their trip onto Chicago. When they arrived in Chicago, they would change trains and have two new Pullman compartments for their trip on to New York City.

Their train travel would be for more than two thousand miles and would take about fifty-five to sixty hours of time.

When they arrived in Kansas City and boarded the train for Chicago, Indian and Serene waited in their compartment with their door open so they would be able to see Tom and White Dove when they boarded the train.

The train was in the station for almost an hour before they began to let the Kansas City passengers come on board the train.

Indian thought as long as it took for the new passengers to get on the train, maybe Robert's parents didn't get to Kansas City in time to meet their train. Then Indian saw a porter bringing Tom and White Dove down the train car aisle to their compartment next door to theirs.

Indian stepped out of their compartment and said, "Hello, Mr. and Mrs. Smiley, I'm glad you made it in time to be on the same train with us.

Tom said, "Indian, how are you? We're glad we made it too. Our train was delayed and just arrived about ten minutes ago."

"I'm sorry you were delayed, but happy you made it in time to go with us."

White Dove asked, "Where's your new wife, Indian?"

"She's right here! After you get settled in your compartment, come over, and I'll introduce her to you."

White Dove replied, "Great, I'm looking forward to meeting her. I understand she is a very close friend of my future daughter-in- law, and I would like to hear more about Joan."

"I'm sure she can tell you all about Joan."

The porter opened their compartment and took their luggage in, and Tom and White Dove followed him into the compartment. Indian and Serene heard the porter leave and close the door to the Smileys' compartment a few minutes later.

About ten minutes later, Indian heard a soft knock on their door, and when he opened the door, he saw Tom and White Dove were standing there.

Indian asked them to come in, and Serene was standing up, waiting for them to come in.

Indian said, "Mr. and Mrs. Smiley, I would like to introduce you to my wife, Serene. Serene, these are Robert's folks, Mr. and Mrs. Smiley."

Tom said, "Serene, I'm Tom, and this is White Dove."

Serene replied, "How do you do? I'm very glad to meet you, Tom and White Dove."

Tom said, "I'm glad to meet you too, Serene. If our son is as lucky as Indian was finding a wife as lovely as you, he will have done very well."

Serene said, "Thank you. I would say Joan is a very beautiful woman, so I think you will find that Robert has done very well."

White Dove asked, "Serene, I understand you met Joan at Vassar College."

"That's correct. We were roommates for four years at Vassar, and our good friend, Latesha, was our other roommate."

White Dove asked, "Serene, you grew up on a ranch in Texas and then you attended Vassar College?"

"That's right, except I also went to boarding school in New York before going to Vassar."

White Dove said, "I wondered how you were able to make it in Vassar, growing up on a ranch in Texas. So, Serene, what kind of a girl is Joan?"

"Joan is a very smart girl, has a great personality, very easy to like, and is just a wonderful friend and person. Your son could never hope to find anyone else as great Joan is."

Tom said, "I can tell you one thing, Robert is crazy in love with her. He says her folks and her brother are just as nice as Joan is. Do you know her parents and her brother at all?"

Serene replied, "Yes, I know them very well. They're wonderful people too. I stayed with them during the summer when I was going to school back east. Joan's mother's name is Patricia Joanna Wagoner Sterling, and her father is a United States senator, Bob Wagoner. As you probably already know, Joan's father's name is John Sterling. He's in the banking business as well as in several other businesses." White Dove said, "We know he's into shipping and the trading business because Robert is running one of the trading companies for him.

We're concerned that because Robert has an Indian mother, he might not be treated very well by his new in-laws."

Serene replied, "I would never be concerned about his in- laws treating him badly. As much as they love Joan, he will be completely accepted into the family. Joan's brother, Michael, is a very nice young man. He's three years older than Joan, and he idolizes her. Joan has run the family since she was five. She might not run their businesses, but if Joan wants it, it's done."

Tom said, "Sounds like a typical American family to me. Daughters usually run the families, whether they're the youngest or the oldest one in the family."

The other three started laughing at Tom's statement because they knew it was true. So the four of them were on their way to New York City.

Indian was the only one who had never been there before, and he was looking forward to seeing this big city.

2

THIS IS NEW YORK CITY

Their train arrived in New York City in the early spring of 1894. Indian, Serene, Tom, and White Dove made their way from the train station to the Waldorf Astoria Hotel.

There, John Sterling had secured suites for them.

The Sterling home was only a few blocks from the hotel, which would be convenient for all the Sterlings' out-of-town guests.

When Indian and Serene arrived in their suite, they had never seen anything like the luxury that they had in this suite. They had a wonderful hotel room in Kansas City, but it wasn't anything compared to the luxury items and furnishing in the Waldorf Astoria. They even had a telephone right in their room. There was champagne on ice and all kinds of snacks, plus fruit, bananas, apples, grapes, and a variety of nuts. The bed had the softest sheets they had ever touched in their life, and the towels were thick and fluffy.

Serene said, "I may never leave here."

Indian responded, "Your cows would sure miss you, and so would I."

"Indian, you know you wouldn't go home without me, would you?"

"My dear Serene, you know I wouldn't, but I'd sure get tired of all these people here in New York."

"Indian, I wasn't talking about staying in New York, just staying in the Waldorf Astoria."

"Maybe you haven't noticed, but the Waldorf Astoria is in the middle of New York City."

"Indian, you take everything I say so literally or that it's just exactly what I mean."

"Serene, you have to remember, I'm just a simple cowboy, and what people say to me is what they mean. Like, I love you means just that, so you have to tell me when you're only kidding about something you say."

"OK, cowboy, I love you so much, and I'm not kidding."

Indian put his arms around her and turned her to be facing him and gave her a huge kiss and said, "I love you so much it hurts sometimes, and if you ever wanted to live in New York, I'd be right here with you."

Indian and Serene lay down on their very large bed, and the telephone rang. Serene got off the bed and answered the telephone, and when she did, she heard Robert say, "Hello, Serene, how was your trip?"

"Robert, you even know how to use a telephone now! And yes, our trip was just fine and certainly at lot easier than it used to be. We can now leave from San Antonio since they have tracks all the way there."

"That's good, Serene, how are my folks?"

"They are just fine, and we enjoyed visiting with them from Kansas City to New York. They are a lot of fun to be with."

"I tried to call them, but they didn't answer the phone, so I thought I would see if you would."

"Robert, would you like me to go knock on the door of their suite? It's just next door to ours."

"I would appreciate it, Serene. I want to be sure they are all right after their trip."

"No problem. I'll let you talk with Indian if he will try talking on the telephone."

Serene said, "Indian, come and talk with Robert while I go see if I can get his folks to answer their telephone."

Indian answered, "OK, if you show me how to use the phone." Indian got off the bed and came around to where Serene was standing, and she handed Indian the receiver and said, "You hold this up to your ear, and you will be able to hear Robert speaking to you, and to talk, you hold the speaker up to your mouth and talk just like you were talking to Robert sitting over there on the couch."

Indian took the receiver and held it up to his ear and then picked up the speaker and said, "Can you hear me, Robert?"

"Sure, I can hear you. How are you, my old friend?"

Although it was the first time Indian had ever talked on a telephone, he didn't feel uncomfortable doing it, so he said, "Where are you, Robert?"

"I'm sitting behind my desk at the trading company."

"Is that all you do, sit behind a desk at the trading company and talk with people on the telephone?"

"Not quite, sometimes I have to get up and fill my own coffee cup if my secretary is busy."

"Man, that sounds like a tough life. You're probably ready to go back chasing cows if you have to get up and get your own coffee."

"Well, I don't have to get it very often, so maybe I better stay here and keep chasing products to import and sell a lot of things we make in America. I'm telling you, Indian, it's a tough life, but somebody has to do it."

"Yeah, Robert, it sounds like it. Wait a minute, here's Serene."

Serene took the phone from Indian and said, "Robert, your folks are OK. Your dad was sleeping and your mother was taking a bath when the phone rang, and by the time your dad woke up enough to answer the phone, it had quit ringing. They're both fine, just a little tired from the trip. Your dad said to tell you to call back in a few minutes and he would love to talk with you, and they are anxious to meet Joan."

Robert replied, "Thanks, Serene. I'll call Dad back in a few minutes. I'm so anxious to see my folks and both of you. Do you know it's been almost three years since I've seen you and Indian and over four years since I've seen my folks?"

"Robert, I know your folks are anxious to see you too, and I know Indian misses you. He's always talking about what the two of you used to do when you were in school."

"Serene, thanks again for checking on my folks. I have to go right now. I need to sign some documents to ship a bunch of things to England. See you all soon. Bye for now."

Serene hung up the telephone and said, "It sounds like Robert is really busy, and he sounded great."

Serene was starting to go over to where Indian was sitting on the bed when the telephone rang again.

Serene picked up the phone and said, "Hello." "Serene, it's Joan. How are you?"

"Joan, it's great to hear your voice. I'm just fine."

"How's Indian, and how is he doing being in the big city?" "He's great, and he hasn't had any problems in New York for the two or three hours we've been here."

Serene could hear Joan laughing at her statement, and finally, Joan said, "How soon can I see you? I can't wait to meet Robert's parents. Would it be all right if I came for dinner tonight with Robert and my folks, so we could see you and Robert's parents?"

"Joan, I don't know why not. We will all love to have dinner. I would think the food would be all right here at the hotel."

"Great, I'll make arrangements for dinner for all of us at the steak house in the Waldorf. You know Latesha is back living in New York, don't you?"

"No, I didn't know that. When did that happen?"

"Serene, you don't know about Latesha being kidnapped in New Orleans?"

"No, when did that happen?" "More than a year ago."

"Is she all right? Is her husband living with her here?"

"Well, Latesha had a pretty tough time recovering since the kidnappers didn't feed her and gave her only a little bit of water. She was in the hospital in Minnesota for several months, but she seems to be completely recovered now. She is still pretty thin, but she looks good."

"I'm so sorry to hear about that. What about her husband? You didn't say if he was living here too."

"Sorry, yes, her husband is living here with her. You have never met Rocky, have you?"

"No, I haven't. What's he like?"

"Rocky is a very nice guy. You know he writes those dime novels, don't you?"

"No, I don't know anything about him."

"As I said, he's a really nice guy. Another of those good-looking cowboys from Texas. However, he wasn't a cowboy, he was a Texas Ranger. After they recovered Latesha, Rocky personally tracked down the man responsible for kidnapping her and killed him."

"Joan, he sounds like he will fit right in with our cowboys. Did you ever imagine when the three of us were going to Vassar that all three of us would marry cowboys? Well, come to think of it, I was pretty sure to marry somebody from the west since I was going back to my daddy's ranch in Texas. Not too many Harvard men in Southeast Texas for me to meet and marry."

"Serene, you got a really good man in Indian." "He's the best."

"OK, Serene, we'll see you all tonight at seven o'clock. Would you be kind enough to tell Robert's folks we will see them for dinner? I'll even bring my brother, Michael. You remember him, don't you?"

"Yes, he's the first man to ever ask me to marry him."

"I know, Serene, and he's a very nice guy too. I guess you broke his heart because he's still not married."

"Goodbye, Joan. We'll see you at seven."

3

DINNER AT THE WALDORF ASTORIA

A few minutes before seven o'clock, Indian, Serene, Tom, and White Dove made their way to the Waldorf Astoria Steak House. Arriving there, they found Joan and Robert waiting at the entrance of the steak house.

Robert took his mother, White Dove, into his arms and gave her a kiss and then hugged his father, Tom, and then shook hands with Indian and gave Serene a hug and a kiss. Robert then introduced his fiancée, Joan Sterling, to his parents. White Dove and Tom both embraced her and told her how much they had been looking forward to meeting her.

Tom said, "We are finally going to get a daughter in this family, we wanted one so much, but we only got Robert."

Everyone laughed, and Joan said, "I want you to know I'm really happy you got him."

Tom replied, "We are too. He's our son, and we think he's a great one too.

Joan agreed, "Robert stole my heart the first time I saw him. I was determined to have him for my husband."

White Dove said, "You know what? He stole my heart the first time I saw him too."

Robert said, "Spoken like a mother."

White Dove replied, "Spoken like a proud mother."

Joan said, "I think we should be seated. I don't know what's happened to my father and mother. They should have been here by now. My brother Michael was going to pick them up on his way here. Anyway, I guess we should be seated and quit blocking the doorway." They were shown to a private dining room where they were seated at a very long table, leaving the head of the table open for Joan's father and on his right, a place for Joan's mother.

They continued talking, and Joan said, "I think we should order drinks and wait to see how long it takes before my folks arrive."

Everyone ordered something to drink, and the conversation continued for another thirty minutes, but still, Joan's parents and her brother hadn't arrived.

Joan said, "There must be something wrong because my father is a stickler about being on time. As he says, 'Not arriving on time for a meeting is insulting to the people you are meeting.' Father is never late. I think I'd better call the house to see what's happened to them."

Robert agreed, "Joan, please do call home to see if something has happened to your father or mother."

Joan left to make a telephone call home. She was gone only for about ten minutes before she came back to the private dining room. Robert saw the anxious look on Joan's face and said, "Joan, what's wrong?"

"Father hasn't returned from a meeting that was scheduled to start at two-thirty this afternoon somewhere at the Port of New York, and he was supposed to be home by around four o'clock. My mother is worried sick. She feels something really bad must have happened to him to be late for dinner and not be here to welcome all of you to New York. She said he was so looking forward to meeting all of you. My brother has contacted everyone who was at the meeting, and they said Father left about three-thirty. They told Michael, Father had planned to take a trolley back home, but no one saw him get on a trolley, so no one knows for sure that he really got on one. Michael said Dad's project planner, Don Evans, who was with Father at the meeting, said everything seemed to be all right with him when he left, and he was looking forward to meeting his soon-to-be new son-in-law's family."

Indian asked, "Is there anything we can do to help locate your father?"

Robert said, "I'm sure Michael is contacting the hospitals and some of Father's people to see if they can find out something. Probably the best thing we can do right now is to go ahead and have some dinner and see if he shows up here after a while, because if he's able, he will be here as soon as he can."

They ordered another round of drinks and dinner, and about the time they were finishing the main course, Michael Sterling arrived at the restaurant. After he had been introduced to everyone, he said, "I've checked all the hospitals in the city and the surrounding areas, and my father has not been admitted to any of them. Frankly, until tomorrow, we don't know anything else we can do. I've contacted everyone we can think of to see if any of them had seen or heard from Father, but no one has. I called the police, but they said they can't make a missing person report until Father has been missing for twenty-four hours. I want you all to know that something really bad has happened to our father or he would have been here to welcome you all to New York. He was looking forward to meeting all of you and to Joan and Robert's wedding. Now, I have no idea what's going to happen about their wedding. I can't see going ahead with it until we can find Father."

Robert and his parents agreed that the wedding would have to wait until they found out what had happened to Joan's father. The evening, which started out so jovial, had quickly turned into a nightmare. What happened to John Sterling and where could he be? Joan said, "I think I need to go home to be with Mother because she is such a worrywart when it comes to Father. She's going to need me with her until we find out what's happened to him. If I find out anything, I will telephone and let you know.

Robert, can you go with us, or do you need to stay with your folks?"

Before Robert could reply, Tom said, "No, Robert doesn't need to stay with us. His place is to be by your side to help you and your mother however he can."

White Dove added, "It's not like we've never been to New York. We went to school here, and Tom's family lived in New York all their lives.

Tom is right. Robert needs to be with you and your family to help anyway he can."

Joan said, "Thank you both. My family really needs him with us. He's a lot tougher than we are. Father sheltered us from the hurts of the real world. We never had to worry about enough to eat or where we were going to live. Whatever problems arrived in our lives or at our doorsteps, Father was always there to fix it or take care of it. We are so spoiled, I don't know how to cook or how to do laundry and ironing. I never even had to make my own bed. Our mother is just like me. She's never had to do any of these things. She doesn't know how and certainly doesn't want to learn now.

As I said, we are very spoiled."

White Dove took Joan into her arms and said, "Honey, you don't have to worry about these things right now. I'm certain your father will be all right, and I'm pretty sure you and your mother are not going to have to start taking in laundry to get by. The kind of a man your father is, I'm sure he has everything set up to take care of your family if something awful has happened to him. I think the best thing you and your brother can do right now is to go home to be with your mother and for all of you to get down on your knees and say your prayers for your father's safe return home. Now, that's something all of us can do right now. Tom, would you lead us in prayer for Mr. Sterling's safety and his return back home?"

"I certainly will. Would all of you join hands together as I say a prayer?"

All the people gathered for dinner joined hands and formed a circle as Tom asked them to do.

Then Tom said, "Father, we thank you for the many blessings you have bestowed on each of your servants in our prayer circle here tonight, and, Father, we beseech you to keep John Sterling safe wherever he is and to swiftly bring him home to his family, friends, and loved ones.

Father, please hear our prayer, and we ask this in the name of your son, Jesus Christ. Amen."

When Tom's prayer ended, the seven people in the circle continued to stand together holding hands until Tom said, "Robert, you need to take Joan and Michael home to be with their mother to comfort her."

Robert let go of Tom's hand, and the rest of the folks in the circle soon let go of everyone else's hands, and each of them were soon on their way to their rooms or to the Sterling home.

4

NEW DAY DAWNS

No one got any sleep in the Sterling home that night, but the sun came up the same way it did every morning. Joan; her brother, Michael; and their mother, Patricia; each took turns pacing around the floor of their library.

Patricia said, "I don't know what we are going to do if we can't find your father before your wedding day, Joan."

Robert said, "Don't worry about that, Mrs. Sterling, our wedding can wait. We have to find Mr. Sterling."

Patricia replied, "But, Robert, your folks are here, and Joan and your friends, the Leaders, have made the trip all the way from Texas for your wedding. I'm sure they can't just stay here a long time. I'm sure they have other things in their lives to do besides sitting around in a hotel waiting."

Robert said, "Mrs. Sterling, we can't spend time worrying about that, we need to find Mr. Sterling. I'm sure something bad has happened to him. He's not one to be late for a meeting of any kind, much less a family gathering. He's told me over and over: the family always has to come first in your life. Nothing else means as much as your family."

Patricia answered, "I know that has always been the way he felt, and I hope that's how you will feel about your wife and family."

"Don't worry, I will, no, that's not true. That's the way I feel already about all of you. You are my family, Mrs. Sterling."

"Robert, will you start calling me either Mom or Patricia? That's enough of calling me Mrs. Sterling."

"OK, Mom, from now on, I will."

Michael said, "Robert, I think you and I should go to the police headquarters and see if they will let us file a report now."

"Michael, I think that's a good idea, and I would like to suggest we call Joan's friend, Latesha Stone, and ask her husband, Rocky, to meet us there. You know he's an ex–Texas Ranger, and I'm sure he will be able to talk to the police about this better than we can."

Joan said, "I'll call Latesha right now."

Joan picked up a telephone and called Latesha's home, and when one of the servants answered the telephone, Joan asked to speak with Latesha.

She was told Miss Latesha and her husband had left home a short time ago to have breakfast with her friend, Serene, and her husband at the Waldorf Astoria. Joan thanked him and hung up the telephone, then she called the Waldorf and asked to speak with Mrs. Serene Leader.

A few minutes passed, and Serene picked up the phone and said, "Hello."

The voice on the other end of the line said, "Serene, this is Joan.

Is Latesha and her husband, Rocky, with you?"

"Yes, they are, they just got here a few minutes ago, and we were about to have breakfast here in our room. I've just introduced them to Indian. Do you want to talk to Latesha?"

"Actually, I would like to talk with Rocky." "OK, I'll give the telephone to him."

Rocky picked up the telephone and said, "Hello, Joan, we're so sorry about your father missing."

"That's what I wanted to talk to you about. Would you meet Michael and Robert at police headquarters to help them fill out a report of Father being missing?"

"Joan, if you think I could be of some help, I'd be glad to." "Rocky, we really do. Being an ex–Texas Ranger, you would know how to talk to policemen better than we would."

"Joan, I speak Texan. I'm not so sure I would be of much help, but I'd be willing to try."

"Great, can you meet Michael and Robert at police headquarters in about an hour?"

"Sure, I'll drag Indian along with us. Remember, he's an ex– deputy sheriff from St. Louis. The New York police might be more impressed with his experience working in a big city than some ex–Texas Ranger."

Rocky hung up the telephone and said, "Indian, I guess we better eat our breakfast. I've just committed us to meet Robert and Michael at police headquarters. Joan has this idea because we're ex–law officers, we can talk to the New York police better than Michael and Robert. I really doubt that, but since Joan is such a good friend of our wives, I told her we would be glad to do it. Sorry if I've committed you to come along with me, considering we just met. I hope you don't mind going along."

"Not a problem, because if we are here, the girls wouldn't be able to have all their girl talk, and we know they are both dying to get started."

Rocky laughed and said, "I think you are probably right." The two women simply smiled.

On the way to the police headquarters, Rocky said, "Indian, how in the world did we get to marry two women who went to school at Vassar?"

"Damned if I know. I think your education is not much more than mine, except you write some damn good books. I couldn't do that. I've read your books for a long time. I never thought I would ever have the chance to meet you. Life sure is funny. Here we are, just a couple of cowboys on our way to the New York City Police Department headquarters to talk about one of the richest men in America being missing for my school friend, Robert's, future in-laws."

Rocky asked, "What kind of a guy is Robert?"

"He is one of the nicest people you will ever meet. Robert's father, Tom, is from New York, and his mother, White Dove, is a Cherokee Indian. They met while going to school to become teachers here in New York. So Robert is one of those mixed-blood people who the world doesn't seem to want to accept for who he is, neither a white man nor an Indian. For one thing, Robert is a big man. He's six foot seven and weighs over three hundred pounds of solid muscle. Robert's nature is as gentle as his mother's name. However, if you were in a fight with a bunch of bad guys, he's the one guy you would want by your side. Robert is also very smart. With his parents both teachers, he was the best educated and smartest kid in school.

No doubt he could have gone to any college in the country, except it's hard to get a mixed-blood person accepted. He came to New York and went to work for his future father-in-law, and he was soon running one of his major companies for him."

When they arrived at police headquarters, they saw Robert and Michael waiting outside for them. Indian introduced Rocky to Robert, and the two shook hands. Rocky thought his hand almost disappeared when he joined his hand with Robert's. Indian was right: Robert was a huge man, and his hand was huge.

Robert asked Rocky if he had met Michael, and he said he hadn't, so Robert introduced him to Michael Sterling. Then the four of them went into police headquarters, and Robert asked to speak to a detective about a missing person. The desk sergeant called someone, and a few minutes passed before a man came up to them and asked if they were the people wanting to talk to a detective about a missing person.

Robert said, "Yes, we are. My name is Robert Smiley, and these are my friends, Michael Sterling, Indian Leader, and Rocky Stone." The detective said, "How do you do? My name is Captain Mitch Wayne. I'm in charge of the division of missing people. How can I help you, gentlemen?"

Michael replied, "We want to report that my father, John Sterling, has been missing since yesterday afternoon."

A young man in the lobby where they were standing overheard the name, stood up, and said, "My name is Ted Washington. I'm with The Sun. Did you say your father's name was John Sterling?"

Michael answered, "Yes, that's right. John Sterling is my father." Ted said, "The John Sterling?"

"Well, yes, I guess he is the John Sterling."

Captain Wayne said, "Gentlemen, I think we'd better go to a conference room."

Ted said, "Just a minute, I want to get some more details about your father being missing."

Captain Wayne said, "Hold on, Teddy. You can get your chance after I get their report."

"Yes, sir, I'll wait until you're finished."

Captain Wayne led them back to a conference room and asked them to have a seat, and he would fill out a missing person report. Captain Wayne asked, "You said your name is Michael Sterling, is that correct?"

Michael replied, "That's right. I'm Michael Sterling, and my father is John Sterling."

"When did you know your father was missing?"

"Yesterday afternoon. He was to be home at five o'clock, and he didn't come home and didn't return home all night."

"Is your father in the habit of coming home at five o'clock every day?"

"No, sir, he normally would be home between six and six-thirty." "How come he was planning on being home at five o'clock yesterday afternoon?"

"Because my sister, Joan, is getting married, and her fiancé's family had just arrived in town, and we were going to meet them for dinner at the Waldorf Astoria at seven o'clock."

"Did your father approve of this wedding?"

"Yes. Robert Smiley is my sister's fiancé, and it was his parents who came from Indian Territory for the wedding."

Captain Wayne turned and looked at Robert and said, "Are you Robert Smiley?"

"Yes, sir."

Captain Wayne asked, "Who are these two other men with you?" Robert replied as he pointed at Indian, "This is my best friend, Indian Leader. We went to school together in Indian Territory. He is to be the best man in my wedding."

Turning his attention to Rocky, Robert said, "Rocky Stone is the husband of my fiancée's best friend, Latesha Stone. You may have read some of his dime novels. He is an ex-captain of the Texas Rangers, and my friend, Indian, is an ex–deputy sheriff of St. Louis County, Missouri."

Captain Wayne looked first at Rocky, then at Indian, and said, "I didn't know I had a couple of ex–lawmen in my meeting. Do either of you have any idea of what's happened to Mr. Sterling?"

Rocky replied, "I have never met the man, and I have only been living in New York for about a year, so I have no idea."

Indian said, "I've never met Mr. Sterling either, and I have no idea of what's happened to him. I only arrived in New York two days ago."

Captain Wayne asked, "How about you, Mr. Smiley? Do you have any ideas?"

"No, sir, I work as the person in charge of Mr. Sterling's import and export business and have worked for him for the past three years. The one thing I know is that Mr. Sterling was a devoted family man, and as he told me, family always has to come first. The other thing I know is that he was at a meeting yesterday somewhere at the Port of New York that started at two-thirty. We know he left the meeting around three-thirty and planned to take a trolley and be home by four o'clock. That's about all I know."

Captain Wayne asked, "Michael, can you add anything to what Mr. Smiley told me?"

"Only that I contacted everyone who was at the meeting yesterday afternoon, and they all confirmed that my father left the meeting at three-thirty and planned to take a trolley home because he had a dinner appointment with his family. Then I contacted all the hospitals in the area and found that he hadn't been admitted to any of the hospitals. We don't know anything else, and we don't have any ideas of where he is or what's happened to him. We only know we need him home."

Captain Wayne said, "I think I have all the information I need to file my report of your father being missing, and we'll do everything we can to help find him so he can return home. You know, we find most of the people who go missing show up in a couple of days, so let's hope that's the case with your father. I would suggest you talk to Teddy Washington with The Sun. A lot of times something in the newspaper helps to find a missing person.

Michael thanked Captain Wayne and promised they would talk with Ted Washington. As they were leaving the building, they found Ted Washington waiting for them in the lobby.

Ted said to Michael, "Do you have time to talk to me now about your father being missing?"

Michael replied, "Yes, we do."

Ted asked, "Would you all like to go across the street and have a cup of coffee or something to drink at the Blue Note Cafe?"

Michael replied, "Sure, I'm pretty thirsty after our meeting with Captain Wayne."

They crossed the street, and the waiter asked, "Your usual table, Teddy?"

Ted replied, "That would be good."

Ted led the way back to a table in the back of the café and took a seat with his back toward the front door. The other four men found seats around the table.

After everyone ordered something to drink, Ted said, "Tell me about your father being missing."

Michael told Ted the same story they had just told Captain Wayne about his missing father. Ted wrote down everything Michael said about what they knew about his father's disappearance. Ted asked almost all the same questions about Mr. Sterling's disappearance that Captain Wayne asked, except Ted asked if Mr. Sterling had a mistress.

This almost caused Michael to lose his composure, but he held himself together and said, "No, my father's never had a mistress."

Ted said, "Sorry, I had to ask that, but so many men in your father's position do have a mistress in this city."

"Well, my father doesn't have a mistress."

Ted said, "I would like to stop by your house and get a recent picture of your father to run in tomorrow's newspaper along with the story. This might help someone to recognize him and cause them to remember if they saw him. The other thing you might want to do is to offer a reward for information leading to his safe return home. You never know how much better people remember if there are dollar signs attached to remembering. At least, it's worth a try."

5

THE NEWSPAPER STORY

Ted Washington stopped by the Sterling home that afternoon and picked up a picture of John Sterling to use in his newspaper article about Mr. Sterling's disappearance. Ted told Michael the article would be printed in tomorrow morning's edition of The Sun.

The next morning, the family gathered around the breakfast table as Michael slowly unfolded the morning edition of The Sun and saw the lead story on the front page was all about one of the richest men in the nation, John Sterling, disappearing a few days before his only daughter's wedding.

The article included his picture and his family's offering a reward of $50,000 for anyone who could help the family locate and bring him safely back home.

At the Waldorf Astoria, Indian and Serene read the newspaper story and hoped someone could help find out what happened to Mr. Sterling.

Serene said, "I wonder how Mrs. Sterling is doing, with her husband missing. I'm sure she is really having a hard time with it, and Joan must be going crazy not knowing if her father is dead or alive. What a horrible thing to happen any time, for your father to disappear, but just before your wedding day, it's got to be tearing Joan apart. I wish I could do something to help her, but I don't have any idea. Do you, Indian?"

"I don't know what you could do unless you could wave a magic wand and bring her father back."

"Well, my magic wand is not working too well, but maybe you and Rocky could do something. You were both law officers. Why don't you two look into his disappearance?"

"My love, my job was usually to arrest someone who was causing a problem to someone or picking up some drunk who was making trouble on the street or in a saloon. I never did much in the way of investigating a crime. I was there to provide a fast gun or some muscle to take someone to boot hill or to jail. I wouldn't know what we should even be looking for."

"Don't sell yourself short, Indian. You've got a good mind, and you'll stay on a job. You may not have the experience doing investigating, but Rocky Stone does. He was the Texas Ranger's chief investigator. Call him and offer to help him look for Mr. Sterling. He would probably be ready to try to find Mr. Sterling or to do something. It might be something he could write up in another one of his dime novels."

"OK, I'm willing to do it, but you would have to place the telephone call because I have no idea how to place one."

"Indian, I'll teach you how to make a telephone call. You just pick up the telephone, take the receiver off the hook, place the receiver up to your ear, and when the woman at the telephone company asks, 'Number, please?' you just tell her the number. Their number is Broadway 600."

Rocky picked up the telephone, took the receiver off the hook, and waited for the telephone operator to ask for the number he was calling, and when she said, "Number, please?" Rocky said, "Broadway 600." He waited a few minutes. He could hear the telephone ringing, and then a man answered the telephone, and Indian said, "May I speak to Rocky Stone, please?"

The man on the other end of the line asked, "Who may I say is calling?"

Indian replied, "Please tell him it's Indian Leader."

"One moment, please, I'll see if Mr. Stone can speak to you now."

A few minutes passed, and Rocky answered the telephone and said, "Hello, Indian, what can I do for you today?"

Indian answered, "Rocky, my good wife has decided that the two of us should try to investigate Mr. Sterling's disappearance. What do you think?"

"Well, I guess it wouldn't be the worst thing that we could do. So if you are willing to try, I'll come over to your hotel, and we'll go see what we can find out."

"Great, come on up when you get here, and if Latesha's not busy, why don't you bring her along, and while we're out playing detectives, the girls can talk or shop or whatever they want to do."

"OK, I'll see you in about an hour."

Rocky hung up the phone and asked Latesha if she wanted to go see Serene while he and Indian were seeing if they could uncover any clue as to what happened to Mr. Sterling. Latesha was keen to do that, so she went with Rocky to the hotel to visit with Serene while their husbands went looking for clues as to what happened to Mr. Sterling. When Rocky and Latesha arrived at Indian and Serene's room, they found Indian ready to go, so after a brief hello to Serene, Rocky and Indian left the hotel.

As they made their way to the Port of New York using trolleys, Rocky asked, "How in the world did you ever get the name Indian?" Indian explained, "I was born in Indian Territory, so my mother named me after the territory. The only reason I know this was because my mother wrote it down in the family Bible. You see, my folks were killed by Indians, and then I was found by some Cherokee Indians and they raised me. I was only about three or four years old when my father found me, that is my Cherokee father. So the only parents that I have ever known were Charlie Whitebird and Moonlight, they're my Pa and Ma. When my Pa found me in the western part of the Indian Territory, I was carrying the Bible that had the name of my parents and my name in it. I was called Indian after finding out that's what it said my name was in my family Bible and what my birth mother had named me: Indian Leader. My birth parents were Irish and English. So I became an orphan when Indians killed my birth parents, and then I was raised by Cherokee Indians." "Thanks, Indian, I had to ask because I never knew or even ever heard of anyone having the first name Indian."

"Well, Rocky, now you have. By the way, did you just name yourself Rocky to go with your last name of Stone to write your books? It is a great name for a writer!"

"No, afraid not. My Pa hung that name on me because he thought it would be funny to give me the name of Rocky Stone. Growing up, lots of people thought my name was pretty funny too. I got into a lot of fights over it."

"I know a little about that. As you know, out west, lots of folks are not happy with Indians because of fighting the Indians. It seems like every family in the west had somebody killed by Indians, including me. My name got me into a few fights as well. I learned just like white people, there were good Indians and bad ones."

They saw that the Port of New York was very busy place indeed. People were loading and unloading cargo and other ships with passengers were getting on and off other ships. Indian had heard about a statue across from the Port of New York called the Statue of Liberty, given to America by France. It was some sight to see.

Indian said, "Rocky, I never thought I would ever see the statue that I read about in our newspaper, and I'm glad I did. I have to say it is very impressive, don't you think?"

"Yes, Indian, that's the same way I felt when I first saw it. It's a sight to behold."

They found lots of newspapers lying around the port with the story of Mr. Sterling going missing while visiting the port. There were also a lot of sailors everywhere. Rocky suggested they try to find people to talk to who worked in the port every day. After talking with several people, they were told they should talk to the stevedores. They were the people who loaded and unloaded the ships, so they were here working every day.

Rocky said, "There's a lot of men loading and unloading ships at this port. Maybe to be able to cover the port quicker, we better split up. You start at one end of the docks and I'll start at the other end, so we can try to talk to as many of these men as we can."

Four hours passed, and neither one of them found out anything except these folks didn't want to talk to anyone about a missing person.

They said they knew nothing about a missing person, and if they did, they wouldn't talk about it to them. The one thing every one of them admitted to was they knew about the $50,000 reward being offered for the finding and the safe return home of Mr. Sterling, and most all of them acknowledged they knew who Mr. Sterling was and would be able to recognize him if they saw him.

Apparently, Mr. Sterling was well-known to the people who worked around the docks. Indian and Rocky spent the whole day and couldn't say they knew any more than they did before they started talking to people.

Rocky said, "You know what I think? We're trying to talk to these men in the wrong place. They not talking when they're working, but they might talk while they were having a drink or two before they went home for the day. Indian, we have to find out where the watering holes are for these men, and then, maybe, they would warm up to us and tell us something about Mr. Sterling."

Indian said, "You know, Rocky, I did hear a couple of men talking about going to their saloons after work. One of the men said something about the Glass Jug and another one talked about going to the Wicked Witch. Those names sound like if we were pouring enough whiskey in those men, we might find out something."

Rocky and Indian decided they should split up again, with one of them going to the Glass Jug and the other one to the Wicked Witch.

Indian said, "I'll take the Wicked Witch because I've worked for a couple of those when I was a cowboy in Texas, so I know how they are."

Rocky laughed and said, "I guess that leaves me with the Glass Jug. I've had lots of experience with men who had emptied too many jugs in my time as a Texas Ranger. So we should be able to handle these joints. However, I don't think we should stay later than seven o'clock, or we might not be able to make it out these joints ourselves."

Indian agreed and said, "I'll meet you at the trolley stop a few minutes after seven."

Rocky headed to the Glass Jug as Indian made his way to the Wicked Witch. When Rocky got to the Glass Jug, he took a seat at the front of the bar and ordered a whiskey and waited to see how many men came by the saloon for a drink before heading home. Not long after five o'clock, the dock workers began coming into the saloon. Rocky struck up a conversation with one of the men he had talked to earlier and found he was happy to tell him what probably happened to Mr. Sterling.

The man said, "My guess is that Mr. Sterling was either hit on the head by some of the thugs that hang around the docks looking for richlooking passengers to roll for their dough or one of the ships who was shorthanded, shanghaied him."

The man said he doubted that Mr. Sterling got shanghaied because he looks too old and too weak to be much use as a deck hand. "Yes, sir, I'd put my money on that he got whacked by the thugs who make their living robbing people around the docks."

By this time, several men had moved up next to the man who was spouting off about his idea of what happened to Mr. Sterling, and they all nodded their head in agreement.

Rocky paid for another round of drinks for the house and thanked the man he had been talking to and said, "Thanks, everyone, for the information. I have to go meet my wife for dinner."

As Rocky walked away from the saloon, he heard the men shouting, "Thank you for the drinks."

Indian's trip to the Wicked Witch saloon resulted in hearing exactly the same thing Rocky heard. All the men who worked the docks believed Mr. Sterling had been hit in the head and robbed by the thugs who worked the docks for a living.

Indian said, "Rocky, I think we need to get back to the hotel, and Serene and I will take you, Latesha, and the Smileys to dinner." "OK, Indian, you've got a deal if you will all come to dinner tomorrow night at our house."

"That sounds like a good deal to me, Rocky."

6

THE LOST OLD MAN

Shannon was making her daily rounds of all the trash barrels located behind the taverns, searching for whatever she could find to eat. When she saw an old man lying behind two of the trash barrels, she wondered if he was dead; he didn't look like he was breathing. She thought, Another old drunk, out of money and out of luck.

She was just beginning to pick through the trash barrel for something to eat when she heard the old man cough and moan. She didn't want to get involved with some old drunk since she had enough troubles of her own. But with her Irish Catholic upbringing, she couldn't just ignore someone who was hurt. She leaned down and touched the old man and asked if he was all right. He turned over on his side to see who was talking to him.

Shannon saw dried blood on the side of his head like he had been hit with something. She said, "Mister, who hit you?"

The old man lay there for a while before answering, and when he did, it was only a whisper. "I don't know. Where am I?"

Shannon said, "You're behind Clancy's Tavern. What happened to you?"

The old man said in the same whisper, "I don't know." Shannon asked, "What's your name?"

The old man said, "I don't know what my name is."

Shannon said, "What do you mean, you don't know your own name?"

The old man said in a louder voice, "I don't know. I just don't know my name. Do you know who I am?"

"Mister, if you don't know your name, how am I supposed to know your name? I don't know your name. Can you get up?"

"I don't know."

The old man turned over on his knees and tried to push himself up from the ground, but he couldn't do it.

Shannon said, "OK, let's see if I can help you up."

Shannon reached her hands down to help him up, and the old man took hold of both of her hands, and she managed to help him to his feet.

When he stood up, his pants began to fall down, but he caught them and pulled them back up.

Shannon asked, "What happened to your belt?" The old man replied, "I have no idea."

"Well, we can't have you walking around town with your pants falling down. I'll find some rope and cut you a piece, and you can use that for a belt."

"Thank you. What's your name, young lady?"

"My name is Shannon McGuire. I'm from Shannon, Ireland. When I was in school, half of the girls in my class were named Shannon, and the other half were named Patricia. So where are you from?"

"I don't know."

"Old man, you don't know nothing, do you?" "No, I guess I don't."

Shannon said, "Well, I'll tell you what I'm going to do. I'm going to give you a name and place you're from. From now on, your name is Michael Gilley, Esquire, from London, England. I gave you that name, because I think if you were cleaned up and had some nice clothes, you would look like one of those proper English gentlemen." The old man replied, "Thank you, Ms. Shannon McGuire. My name is Michael Gilley, Esquire, from London, England, and I'm very glad to meet you."

Shannon replied, "Thank you, kind sir. Now I shall go find you a piece of rope, so you can walk without having your pants falling down."

In spite of the pain in his head, the old man said with a slight laugh, "That would be so kind of you, Ms. Shannon McGuire."

Shannon left, and in a few minutes, she returned with a piece of rope for Michael's pants. Michael had no idea where she got the rope, but he was glad she did. After she helped him feed the rope through his pant loops, she helped him tie the rope tight enough to hold his pants up.

Then she said, "I guess you're hungry too, aren't you?"

Michael replied, "Yes, I guess I am. It seems like I was on my way to have dinner when something happened to me and I never made it. Where are we going to go to have something to eat?"

"Well, when I found you, I was just beginning to search for something to eat, so I guess we should go back to Clancy's Tavern's trash barrels to see what we can find."

Michael asked, "You mean you don't have a place to live and you don't have any money?"

"I'm afraid not. I have a box down behind the docks to live in, but I sure don't have any money and I can't get a job. So, Michael, do you have some money?"

"Well, I think I do."

Michael put his hand in his pockets and found he had nothing in them.

Michael said, "I guess I don't have any money or anything else." Shannon said, "Come along, we'll see what we can find."

The two of them went back behind Clancy's Tavern, and Shannon began looking through the trash barrels for something for them to eat. She soon found a half loaf of hard bread and part of a chicken and put them in a cloth sack she took out of her pocket.

Then Shannon said, "OK, we'll go on to Bob's Place and see what we can find there."

Michael tagged along behind her, keeping up the best he could; she walked very fast and told Michael he would have to keep up with her.

She said, "We have to get back to my box before it gets dark. Otherwise, somebody else will get my box for the night."

Michael was hurrying as fast as he could, but the best he could do was to keep her in sight. She stopped to look through the trash barrels at Bob's Place, and there, she found a half-eaten piece of roast beef, some boiled potatoes, and some carrots. She was then off to her next stop, the Golden Cow, where she found another piece of roast beef, a ham bone with a lots of meat left on it, and a couple of half-rotten apples.

Shannon said, "Michael, this should keep us fed for tonight, and tomorrow, we'll have to expand my hunting ground to be able to find enough food for the two of us."

The two of them kept walking until they were down on the fishing boat docks, and Shannon stopped at one of the fish- cleaning stations located on these docks. She found some rags which had been left there by some fisherman. She turned on the water and told Michael to come over by her so she could wash the dried blood from his head. Michael did as she asked, and Shannon washed away the blood and cleaned his head and face.

Michael said, "I don't think anyone has washed my face for me since my mother did when I was a child. Thank you, Shannon."

Shannon replied, "Well, I got tired of looking at your dirty, bloody face. You know, with a clean face, you're a rather handsome man."

"Thank you, Shannon. Why are you helping me?"

"I have two reasons for helping you: first, because of my Irish Catholic upbringing, and second, because if you're with me, maybe you can help me keep the men away who have been trying to force themselves on me to get into my knickers. With the help of Little Red, I've been able to keep one of them off me, but I'm not so sure I could if there were two or more men. I plan to tell everyone you're my stepfather. You understand why I'm helping you now?"

"I do. How come you're in this town if you're from Shannon, Ireland?"

"You want to know my sad tale of woe, do you? Let's just say I came to New York to get married to the boy from Ireland I was to marry, who came to America to make a better life for us. But when I got here, I found out he got some Italian girl pregnant and her Pa made him marry her, and when I went to where I was supposed to live with him, his new wife told me to get lost. So here I am, with no one to look after me, no place to live, no money to go back home, and I can't find a job. When I ask for a job, they tell me they don't hire any Irish women. What I brought with me from home, I had to sell to get something to eat, and the rest of my things were stolen from me after I ended up here on the docks. That's my fine tale of woe."

"Shannon, what's this Little Red you've been using to protect yourself from these men who have tried to rape you?"

Shannon reached into her cloth bag and pulled out a knife that was about six inches long. After the blade was opened and locked, she told Michael, "This is Little Red. My grandmother, well, she wasn't really my grandmother but I called her my grandmother, gave it to me to protect me from the Indians in America. I haven't seen any Indians, but so far, it has protected me from these bums who live around the docks."

"OK, thank you, Shannon."

Then Shannon made a fire with some dried wood she had collected, took a pot she had gotten from somewhere, and made a pot of stew out of the roast beef, ham bone, potatoes, and carrots. She trimmed off the rotten part of the two apples and washed offwhat was left of them. After everything was cooked, she got out two bowls and two spoons and served a bowl to Michael and one to herself.

Michael said, "It's the finest bowl of stew I've ever had."

After they finished their stew and ate their half of their apple, they took everything down to the fish-cleaning station and washed their dishes.

When they returned to Shannon's box home, they lay down and went to sleep, with Michael on the outside of the box and Shannon on the inside of the box.

Shannon had the best night of sleep she had since her arrival in America.

7

THE SEARCH GOES ON

The next morning, Rocky telephoned Indian and asked him if he wanted to continue to help him search the waterfront to see if they could find out anything about Mr. Sterling.

Indian said yes and suggested they should try to find out if there was a lot of crime that went on around the docks. If there was, maybe they could find out if one or more of the crooks attacked Mr. Sterling and what they did with him.

When they arrived at the docks, Rocky began talking with several of the people who worked at the offices, asking them if they thought there was a lot of crime that occurred in the area. The answer was a resounding yes, and they felt crime was awful, and many said they hated to have to come to work here and would never stay late in the evening.

Rocky said, "Indian, I think we should find someplace where we could just watch to see what goes on around here for awhile."

Rocky and Indian found the Harbor View Café where they could sit outside with a wide view of the area where passengers were getting on and off the ships. They ordered coffee and begin watching as people were walking to and from the ship's docks. Only a few minutes passed before they saw a well-dressed man and woman who were just coming into the city, then they saw two rough-looking men approach the couple, and one of the men pulled a gun and stopped them. The other tough-looking man took the woman's purse, looked through it, and took out all the money and jewelry out of the purse. Next, he had the man give him his wallet, and then he emptied the wallet of all its contents into a bag the robber was carrying. The two bandits then turned to go as the couple just stood there and watched as the bandits ran away into some nearby trees.

Rocky and Indian slowly got up from their table and very deliberately began walking in the general direction the two bandits had gone. But instead of going directly into the grove of trees where the bandits went, Rocky and Indian split up, one going around the grove of trees on one side and the other one going around to the other side of the grove of trees. After they made the circle around the trees, together, they slowly and quietly started into the grove with their guns drawn. They saw the two bandits sitting on the ground counting and dividing up the money they had just taken from the couple.

Rocky said, "Put your hands above your head. Otherwise, you don't move.

The bandits looked up and saw Rocky with his gun pointing at them, and a little way from him, they saw Indian standing with his gun aimed at them. They both put their hands in the air as Rocky had told them. Indian walked over to the two bandits and reached down and took the man's gun from his coat pocket, then told him to stand up.

When the man stood up, Indian put the gun barrel against his belly and asked, "Did you and your partner rob a well-dressed man a few days ago while he was waiting for a trolley?"

The man replied, "I have no idea what you're talking about. We ain't robbed nobody."

With that, Indian whacked the man on the side of his head and the man went down on his knees.

Indian said, "You ain't robbed nobody? That slight tap on your head is for lying to us. We just watched you rob that nice couple. The next time you lie to me, you'll get more than a tap on your head."

The other man, still sitting on the ground, said, "I don't know who you cowboys are, but you better back off 'cause you don't know who we work for."

Rocky said, "I guess you better tell us who you work for before I let my partner cut you up in little pieces. You know, he was raised by Indians.

Do you have any idea what Indians would do to you if they caught you lying to them? Believe me, you don't want to know."

The bandit, still sitting on the ground, shouted, "We work for Don San Marco, you've heard of him, haven't you? He controls all the area around the docks. Nobody works around here without paying him or you come up dead."

Rocky said, "Well, we would like to meet this Don San Marco. We think somebody messed with one of our friends when he was down here a few days ago, and we don't like it. Now, he's missing, and nobody around here is going to be operating business as usual until we find our friend or lots of Don San Marco's people are going to wind up dead. You tell him if he wants to meet to talk about it, he can meet us tomorrow morning at ten o'clock at the Harbor View Café. You get my meaning, friend? His people are going to be dead! We can start with you two, if you like. Empty your pockets of everything you have in them. You walk away with nothing."

The two bandits took everything out of their pockets and put it on the ground along with the money they took from the couple they just robbed.

Indian said, "Now get the hell out of here and don't look back." The two bandits walked out of the grove of trees, and Indian picked up all the money and the things the bandits left and picked up the man's gun and put it in his coat pocket. Then Rocky and Indian walked down to the dock, found the couple the bandits had robbed and gave them back all their money and jewelry the bandits had taken, plus whatever other money Rocky and Indian took from the bandits.

The couple thanked them and said, "You've given us back more money than the bandits took from us."

Indian said, "Just say it's a little extra for causing you folks so much trouble."

Rocky and Indian then made their way up to the nearby trolley stop and stood inside a small shop, waiting to see if anything might happen here.

They saw a well-dressed gentleman approach the trolley stop when two men stepped out of an alleyway and grabbed him and were attempting to take his wallet. Suddenly, the two men felt a gun against their backs and released the man. Rocky took the wallet from the bandit and handed it back to the well-dressed man, and the trolley pulled up to the stop.

The well-dressed man got aboard and said, "Thank you." Indian said, "We're glad to be of service to you, friend."

Indian said to the two bandits, "You men work here a lot, do you? Did you rob an older well-dressed man here a couple of days ago? We're looking for our friend who has been missing for a few days. If you know what happened to him, we would appreciate your help in finding him, or we can make some arrangements for your funerals."

One of the bandits said, "No way, man. We just had to have a little money to get a drink, and that guy looked like he could spare a little money. We got to have a drink, and we don't have any money." Indian said, "You need a drink, and you don't have any money, huh? Put your hands in your pockets and take everything out of them, and be really careful what you pull out because my friend really likes to shoot people, and he hasn't had the chance to shoot anybody all day."

The two bandits put their hands in their pockets and turned them inside out. Big surprise, money came tumbling out, falling to the ground, and Indian whacked the man who said they had no money right across the face with his gun barrel.

The man fell to the ground, and Indian said, "That's for lying to me. Now get yourself up and go tell your boss, Don San Marco, that his people are out of business around the docks until we find our friend. You tell him if he wants to talk, to meet us at the Harbor View Café at ten o'clock tomorrow morning. Do you understand me? Now get the hell out of here before we change our mind and blow both of you away."

Rocky said, "I think we should find out who is in charge of the dock area and see what he knows about the crime they have around here and why the police are not doing a better job of protecting the visitors and the workers."

"Sounds like a good idea to me, Rocky. Let's see if we can talk to him."

They walked back down to the docks and asked one of the people, who sold tickets for the ships, who was in charge of the dock area.

The ticket seller said, "Mr. Burt Wilson, he's the harbor master, and his office is the next building over from here."

Rocky and Indian walked next door to Mr. Burt Wilson's office, and when they got to the office, they were greeted by a nice- looking young woman who asked if she could help them.

Rocky said, "We would like to meet with Mr. Wilson about a security issue around the dock area."

The young woman said, "Oh, you mean the lack of any security around here."

Indian replied, "Well, that's kind of what we wanted to ask him about."

"I'll see if Mr. Wilson is about finished with his meeting with one of the ship's captains."

The young woman opened the door to Mr. Wilson's office, and after a couple of minutes, she and a man came out of his office. She said, "Gentlemen, you may go in to see Mr. Wilson now."

Rocky and Indian walked into Wilson's office and found Mr. Wilson puffing on a big cigar, and he said, "I'm Burt Wilson. What can I do for you, men?"

Rocky replied, "Mr. Wilson, my name is Rocky Stone, and this is my friend, Indian Leader, and we would like to hear what you think about the security for your passengers and employees in the dock area."

Wilson replied, "What security? We don't have any security for our passengers or employees. The damn police captain responsible for the dock area refuses to provide any police protection for our people. He says they just don't have enough men to patrol the dock area with everything else they have to look after in this part of the city. So there you have it, gentlemen, no security whatsoever."

Rocky said, "I want to tell you, sir, crime is running rampant in your area, and it looks to me like you have the responsibility to provide a safe, secure area for your passengers and employees."

"If the police captain can't provide police officers to patrol our area, what in the hell do you think I can do?"

Indian said, "Then, Mr. Wilson, you need to have your own police department for the dock area."

"How could I do that?"

Rocky said, "You hire someone who has police experience and someone who has supervised police officers to establish your own department, you know, like the Harbor Police."

Mr. Wilson looked at Rocky and Indian and said, "Gentlemen, you have a great idea. So how did you come up with this idea?"

Rocky replied, "We have a friend who was at a meeting here a few days ago who disappeared and never returned home after his meeting. Since both of us have been law enforcement officers in the past, we decided to come down to the dock area and see if we could find our friend. We have been here in the dock area for a few hours, and in that time, we have stopped two robberies and got the people's money and things back for them."

Wilson's said, "Unbelievable, what were your names again?"

Rocky answered, "My name is Rocky Stone. I used to be the chief investigator for the Texas Rangers. My friend's name is Indian Leader, who has experience as deputy sheriff of St. Louis County, Missouri. We're here in town for a friend's wedding, and the father of the bride, Michael Sterling, was attending a meeting here a few days go and never made it back home after the meeting."

"Oh, yes, I know Mr. Sterling, a fine man, and yes, he was here. We were going over plans for the dock area for the future. It's just awful him disappearing like that."

Indian said, "Well, that's the reason we are here, looking around for any clues as to what happened to him."

Wilson said, "I would do anything I can do to help you find Mr. Sterling. I understand you are in town for his daughter's wedding, but would you consider helping me bring your idea of establishing a Harbor Police into a reality?"

Rocky and Indian were taken aback by Mr. Wilson's suggestion that they help him establish a Harbor Police Department. Indian looked at Rocky, who stared back at him and finally Rocky replied, "Well, I guess we would consider temporarily helping you form a Harbor Police Department, wouldn't we, Indian?"

"I guess while we are here, we would be glad to help you. Maybe, Rocky, you could get an idea for writing another book doing it."

Mr. Wilson said, "Great. The City of New York will be grateful for your service in establishing the Harbor Police Department. One question, Rocky, are you the man who writes those dime novels? I love your stories. I'm sure I have every one you've ever written."

Rocky answered, "I'm the guilty one. I wrote all those books." Wilson said, "OK, now that you gentlemen are going to start a police department for me, I need to officially appoint you to your positions. Rocky, I want to name you chief of the Harbor Police Department and, Indian, you are the captain of the department. Since we don't have badges, I will have papers made up showing you as chief and captain of the Harbor Police Department. The two of you, of course, will be paid for your services, and it will be up to you to find the people to take your positions and hire other police officers. My secretary can take care of getting you whatever you need. We'll find you a building for the office of the Harbor Police Department and build a jail in it to hold prisoners. Gentlemen, the rest, as they say, is up to you. Congratulations, Chief Stone and Captain Leader, welcome to the service of the New York City's Harbor Police Department."

Mr. Wilson shook hands with both of them and told his secretary to make the documents for the chief of New York City Harbor Police Department, Rocky Stone, and captain of the New York City Harbor Police Department, Indian Leader. The secretary made the documents and handed them to Mr. Wilson to sign, which he did, and then he handed them to Rocky and Indian.

Rocky and Indian walked out of Mr. Wilson's office, and Indian said,

"What did we just do to get us into this mess?"

Rocky replied, "I'm not sure, and I don't know what we're going to tell our wives what we gotten ourselves into."

8

NEW DAY ON THE HARBOR

Rocky and Indian's wives were really not happy to hear that Rocky and Indian had taking on the responsibilities of establishing a Harbor Police Department for the City of New York. To say they were not happy about the news was one of the understatements of the year. They were mad as hell!

The words were something like, "What were you thinking? Are you out of your minds?" Anyway, it was something like that.

Rocky just said, "Honey, it just a temporary job, and I thought we could help protect a lot of nice people who are traveling in and out of New York."

Latesha replied, "Why does it have to be you?"

"Well, somebody has to do it, and remember, Indian is helping me." Almost the same conversation was taking place in Indian and Serene's Waldorf Astoria hotel suite.

Serene said, "Indian, what in the world were you thinking? You don't have time to help New York start a Harbor Police Department. We have to get back to the Star Ranch as soon as we can get Joan and Robert married.

Our ranch is what our job is, not looking after the people who use the New York City Harbor. I know how you are, always wanting to help everybody.

I've got news for you, love, you can't fix everything for everybody in this bloody world."

"Serene, we're not trying to help everyone in the whole world, just the people who use the harbor in New York City. I'm not doing it by myself, Rocky's helping me."

No amount of words were going to satisfy Rocky's and Indian's wives; they didn't want their husbands involved in starting a police department for New York's City's Harbor. However, Rocky and Indian had already given their word, and when cowboys give their word to do something, no matter what their wives say, they were going to do it or die trying.

But on the other hand, that was one of the things their wives loved about them, so in the end, they both knew Rocky and Indian were starting a Harbor Police Department for the City of New York. Rocky met Indian at the hotel, and they made their way to the harbor to begin their task of putting together a Harbor Police Department, regardless of what their wives had to say.

Rocky asked Indian, "So how did it go with Serene when you told her of our new job?"

"Oh, I would say about the same way it went when you told Latesha."

Rocky replied, "That good, huh?" "Maybe not quite that good."

When they arrived at the harbor master's office the next morning they talked with his secretary, Daisy Johnson, and asked her to find out who supplied the New York City Police Department with their uniforms and badges. Their next stop was to meet with Don San Marco at the Harbor View Café at ten o'clock. They were looking forward to this meeting to see what kind of person this man was. They didn't know what to expect since they had no idea what he looked like or if they should be ready to kill the man on the spot.

They took a table where they had their backs against a wall, where no one could shoot them in the back while they were talking to this Don San Marco.

They didn't think he would have any trouble finding them in the café since they would be the only ones who looked like a couple of cowboys, dressed in their cowboy clothes. They both had their .44s in their lap, with their right hand on them, ready for whatever Don San

Marco's play might be. What they soon found out was nothing like anything they had ever been up against in their lives.

Don San Marco came into the café by himself, dressed in one of the finest tailored suits they had ever seen in their lives. Don San Marco had a neatly trimmed beard and mustache, with piercing brown eyes, and carried a cane, which was obviously for appearance, not because he needed it to walk. They would find out later that his cane had a sinister secret.

They thought he looked to be around forty years old, about five footseven, and must have only weighed about a hundred and fifty pounds. He looked trim and fit. When he spoke to them, he spoke in broken English, and his speech was almost a whisper.

"Gentlemen, I'm Don San Marco. You wanted to see me?"

Rocky spoke first and said, "We understand you are the boss of these bandits who work the dock area of New York."

"Maybe so."

Indian spoke next, "Don San Marco, we asked for this meeting because we think some of your people may have harmed a friend of ours three days ago as he was waiting for a trolley. We think they may have killed him because he hasn't made it home yet. We want to know where he is, and we're going to shut down your business in the dock area of New York, so you might as well take your people and take your business somewhere else."

"You two cowboys are going to shut my business? I don't think so. You can be dead tomorrow."

Rocky replied, "Well, Don San Marco, you could be dead today, if you know what I mean."

"Maybe, but you could never get out of this café alive either." Rocky asked, "Don San Marco, can you read English?"

"Of course, I read English."

Rocky said, "Then you can read this."

Rocky took his new ID paper out of his pocket and laid it down in front of Don San Marco.

Don San Marco looked the paper over and said, "It looks like you can be a target every day from now on. You're just a dead man still walking around today."

Rocky replied, "Well, Don San Marco, I guess that makes two of us, you and me."

Indian spoke up and said, "Don San Marco, you have been warned to take your gang out of the dock area, or you and your men will be targeted every day and night. You have to remember, we're only cowboys, and we live by the code of the west: you try to kill us, we will kill you and your men."

Don San Marco got up from the table and said, "OK, you have warned me, now I'm warning you. Every one of your men will be a target for us every day."

Rocky said, "Don San Marco, you can walk out of this café right now, but the next time I see you, we will arrest you or you can die trying to get away. Go, right now, and take your gang with you. Get out of the dock area."

Don San Marco turned and began walking out the café, and Indian said, "I think we should have taken him out right now. He's not the kind you can threaten to get him to do something, you have to kill him."

"OK, Indian, I won't make that mistake again. Indian, since you had a lot more experience working in St. Louis, the largest city in the west, you need to guide me as to what we need to do to protect and patrol the dock area of New York."

"Rocky, what we have to do is to hire enough men to operate twenty- four hours, seven days a week, by working three shifts. Shift 1 would work from 7:00 a.m. to 3:00 p.m. Shift 2 works from 3:00 to 11:00 p.m., and shift 3 works from 11:00 p.m. to 7:00 a.m. Plus, we must have enough men to give everyone off at least one day a week. Rocky, who do you think would make good police officers?" "I would say someone who could handle themselves in a fight." "You know, Rocky, I've heard the Irish love to have a good fight now and again and then can go have a couple of pints together and be friends. I've never known any Irish men personally, but I see those signs around town advertising for help that say, no Irish need apply.

So I think we should make up signs for our employees that say, Irish are welcome to apply."

Rocky and Indian went back to the harbor master's office, and Daisy had the information they asked for about who supplied the New York City Police Department uniforms and badges. Daisy told them they would need purchase orders signed by the harbor master in order for them to buy the equipment they needed. Then she handed Rocky four signed purchase orders made out to the companies that supplied uniforms, badges, weapons, and other police equipment and one for office equipment.

Indian said, "Rocky, why don't you take care of all these items, and I'll work at getting signs made up to hire police officers and hire the men."

"Sounds like a deal to me."

Rocky left to see about buying all the equipment they needed as Indian went to make up signs to hire police officers and put them out so people could see them. By the end of the day, Rocky had made arrangements for uniforms, badges, police weapons, and police equipment their officers would need: nightsticks, handcuffs, and office equipment and supplies.

At the same time, Indian had his signs made up and posted them in all the saloons and several businesses in the area near the docks. The signs stated anyone interested in becoming a Harbor police officer was invited to begin inquiring at the harbor master's office at nine o'clock the next morning.

Before six o'clock the next morning, men were lining up outside the harbor master's office. When Indian arrived a little before nine o'clock, he saw they had over a hundred men in line waiting to be interviewed for the position of a Harbor police officer. By ten-thirty, Indian had hired thirty men for the jobs and still needed to hire at least another thirty. By four o'clock that afternoon, Indian had hired seventy-five men to be Harbor police officers. Almost all the men hired were from Ireland and had come to America to find a better life for themselves and their family and then found they couldn't get a job because they were Irish. Six of the men were from Italy and when asked, they all said they knew who Don San Marco was, and all of them said he was bad news and gave Italians a bad name, so they hoped they could help stop his criminal activates in the dock area.

One of the men from Ireland had served as a police officer in Dublin and held the rank of captain until he arrested a local judge for beating his wife and had almost killed her. He was fired because his superiors told him a man had the right to whip his wife if she wasn't behaving herself the way her husband wanted. It seemed the man, Sean O'Malley, didn't think that was right and punched out his commanding officer.

Indian thought Sean would make a good man to be in charge of one of the shifts and planned to tell Rocky they should give him the rank of lieutenant in charge of the third shift. He also thought Sean could help with the training of the new police officers. Before the day was over, Rocky and Indian had their badges and appointments the next day for their uniforms.

Indian talked to Rocky about Sean, and he agreed with Indian that they should make him a lieutenant in charge of the third shift and help them with the training of the other men as police officers. That night, Rocky and Indian and their wives had dinner together, and after dinner, they put together a training schedule for their new recruits while their wives talked about what was ever going to be done about Joan and Robert's wedding.

The following day, Rocky had his appointment to get his uniform while Indian and Sean started the training classes for the new police officers. Rocky returned that afternoon in his new uniform: a navy-blue coat and pants with a gold stripe down the side and a cap in the same navy blue, with a badge that said New York City Harbor Police. The badge on his chest read the same way: New York City Harbor Police Chief. This would be the model for all the police officers' uniforms, except their badges would indicate their rank, from patrolman to chief.

That afternoon, Indian went to the uniform shop and got his new uniform that was just like the one for Rocky, except his badge said Captain.

Each day for the next two weeks, the training of the new police officers would continue, and each of the new men would go to get their new uniforms. At the end of the two weeks' training period, they were ready to begin walking their various beats. The officers would work in pairs, and each officer was issued a whistle to blow in case they needed help. Any of the other officers in the area should immediately go to aid any officer that needed help if they heard an alarm whistle. The first day, everything seemed to work pretty well. The shifts had little or no problems as Rocky, Indian, and Sean worked around the area being patrolled for all three shifts.

The same for the next day: with Rocky working with the first shift, Indian with the second shift, and Sean working with the third shift. Reports of crime in the dock area dropped as soon as the officers began patrolling the area. Rocky and Indian didn't know what Don San Marco and his men were doing now, but they seemed to have moved their operation out of the dock area. They only hoped it stayed that way.

Every day, they tried to find out what had happened to Michael Sterling by talking to people who worked in the dock area, and after two weeks, they knew no more than they did the first day they came to the dock area. Rocky and Indian were convinced someone in this dock area knew what happened to Michael Sterling, and they still planned to find him.

9

LIVING ON NOTHING

At the end of the second week of Shannon and Michael being together and living on the dock area of New York City, they found they worked well together. It seemed Michael had a lot of luck finding ways of making a little money. He got paid to sweep off the sidewalks in front of some of the many saloons in the area and got Shannon and himself work washing dishes at Bob's Place whenever the regular dishwasher was too drunk to come to work.

Michael made more money by helping people carry their luggage down to the ships and out from the ships to the trolleys. They were earning enough money that they could actually buy food and didn't have to eat out of trash cans anymore, and they were able to buy some used clothes for each of them. Michael even had a belt now to hold up his pants.

Michael had let his beard grow out, so his appearance didn't look like he did when he first began living with Shannon. She told him he looked much nicer with his beard now that she was able to keep it trimmed for him.

Michael had been clean shaven his entire life, but now he didn't have a razor or shaving soap, so the beard worked all right for him.

When he saw himself in the mirror, he thought he looked like one of those ship captains they were always using in ads for various products.

He also thought his white beard made him look much older.

They still lived in Shannon's box home, as they called it, and no one had attempted to molest Shannon since Michael came into her life. One day, Michael saw an advertisement for an office worker for the new Harbor Police Department, and it even said Irish were welcome to apply.

Michael said, "Shannon, why don't you apply for this job?" "Oh, they wouldn't employ me. I'm Irish."

Michael replied, "The sign said Irish are welcome to apply." "Look at me. Do I look like I'm someone who could work in an office?"

"And just what does a woman who works in an office look like?" "They look like they had their hair clean and combed with decentlooking clothes to wear and a clean face and body. They would even smell good, not the way I smell."

"Shannon, let's take the money we have to get you a bath, a haircut and style for your hair, and then buy you a nice used dress to wear to apply for the job. We know where you can get a bath and cleaned up for not much money, and the nice lady who works there can cut and fix your hair. Then we'll go to the thrift shop, and I'll help you find a dress that will get you that job. One other thing I need to ask, do you know anything about working in an office?"

"I guess I do. I worked in the office at school for four years. I was going to be a bookkeeper when I finished school."

"So in other words, you've got four years of experience working in an office."

"Well, I guess I do."

"Shannon, have a little confidence in yourself. You can get this job and get out of living in a box down on the dock. You can do it."

"Thanks, Michael, maybe I can."

"No maybe. Shannon, you can do it. Let's go get you the dress you need to get the job and then get you cleaned up and shining like a new penny."

"OK, Michael, if you think I can do it, I can."

They walked to the thrift store and the lady working there helped Shannon find a nice-looking dress and showed it to Michael, but he said, "No, it's too bright, she has to have something that looks like she means business."

Finally, the lady brought out a black tailored dress that looked like it would fit Shannon, and Michael said, "That's what you need, but you need shoes to go with the dress."

The lady found a pair that worked perfectly with the dress. They bought the dress and shoes and then went to the public bathhouse where Shannon had a very long hot bath and washed her hair. Then the lady at the bathhouse cut and fixed her hair for her.

When Shannon came out clean with her hair fixed and wearing her new dress and shoes, Michael said, "My daughter, that's the way you should look every day. You look beautiful."

When Shannon saw herself in the long mirror, she had to take a second look to be sure it was her reflection in the mirror that she was seeing.

To her surprise, it was!

Michael marched her down to the new Harbor Police Department station and sat down on a bench outside and said, "OK, Shannon, go in there and get the job."

Shannon pulled her shoulders back and opened the door to the police station and walked in like she owned the place.

Twenty minutes later, Shannon came out and said, "I got the job, Michael."

"Of course you did, my love, they had to hire you."

Shannon said, "The very nice man who interviewed me had the funniest name. You are never going to believe it. You couldn't ever guess what his name was."

"OK, I can't guess his name. What was it?"

"He said his name is Indian Leader. Can you believe it?" "You're right. I never would have guessed it. What a strange name."

Shannon said, "Well, his name might be strange, but he was a very nice man, and he liked me right off and told me I would like working there because they had so many men working there from Ireland. He said, I'll think I'm back home in Ireland. I guess they think Irish men will make good police officers."

"So when do you start to work, Shannon?"

"Tomorrow at seven o'clock in the morning. Then I get off at three p.m.

"That sounds wonderful, Shannon. We better go find you another work dress. You can't come to work your first day in the same dress you wore for your interview."

"Michael, you sure seem to know a lot about what women should wear to work."

"I don't know, Shannon, maybe I used to work in an office." "Maybe you had a wife or a daughter who worked in an office." "If I did, you would think I would remember them, wouldn't you?" "I don't know, with the hit on your head, who knows what happened to your memory. You might be someone who goes around killing people, and you don't want to remember who you used to be. All I know is you're Michael Gilley, Esquire, from London, England. You're my friend and one of the kindest people I've ever met. You make me feel very special, and I love you more than my own father, whom I never knew. My father and I certainly never slept together in a box house on the docks of New York City. However, whoever you are, you're a wonderful man, and you've saved my life."

"Well, Ms. Shannon McGuire, you certainly saved my life, and you make the best Irish stew I'm ever had in my life. I love you as if you were my daughter."

They spent the last of the money for Shannon's work dress and dinner that night at Bob's Place. After they finished their dinner, Bob said, "Michael, I would like to hire you to be my steady dishwasher starting tomorrow. I finally gave up on Freddy because he came to work drunk again tonight."

"That sounds good, Bob. I'll see you in the morning, at what time?"

"Eight o'clock will be fine."

"Thank you, Bob. I'll see you in the morning."

When they left Bob's Place, Michael said, "Tomorrow, let's see if we can find a cheap place to live, one that might even have a bath and indoor toilet."

"I know we both have jobs now, but where are we going to get the money to pay the first month's rent?"

Michael replied, "I'm pretty sure Bob will be willing to give me an advance to get us someplace to live after I tell him we've being living in a box down on the fishing docks."

"I hope you can get him to do that, no, wait, I'm sure you can get him to do that."

After work the next afternoon, Michael and Shannon began their hunt for someplace to live and found a small two-room apartment that had a bathroom they could share with four other people who lived in two other apartments in the building. Bob had given Michael an advance on his salary, so they were able to pay a month's rent in advance and to move in that very afternoon.

After they gathered up their few belongings from their box house, Michael said, "You know, I'm going to miss living here."

"Oh, Michael, you are so silly. How can you say you're going to miss living in a box on fishermen's dock?"

"Well, Shannon, I didn't say I was going to miss it much, but it was our first home together."

Shannon said, "It probably won't be our last home together. I'm never going to let you go out of my life. I love you too much, and we've been through so much together."

"Shannon, I feel the same way about you, and you've done so much to look after me. I love you too."

The next day, they both went to their new jobs, and Indian was right in what he told Shannon, everybody she met was from Ireland. One of the men she met was the first day was in charge of the night shift, and she thought he was one of the best-looking men she had ever met in her life; his name was Sean O'Malley.

She thought, I hope he likes me because I could really go for him. One of the men getting off work from the third shift made a smart remark to Shannon, something like "How'd you like to come home with me, baby?"

Sean immediately said, "Officer Toomey, we'll have none of that kind of talk to an employee in this department."

Officer Toomey replied, "Yes, sir. Miss, I want to apologize to you for what I said. I'm very sorry."

Shannon gracefully replied, "Thank you, Officer Toomey. I accept your apology, no more needs to be said."

Both Officer Toomey and Sean smiled at Shannon.

Then Sean asked, "Miss, for the record, we should know your name, so we know how to address you."

"My name is Miss Shannon McGuire, from Shannon, Ireland, and I have only been in America for about six months, and I'm very glad to have this job and be working with a fine group of Irish lads. It makes me feel like I'm home."

Sean said, "Well, Ms. McGuire, I can assure you, you're not in Ireland anymore, and I have to ask if you started going to church here yet.

I find too many of our folks have forgotten our roots once they came to America. How about you?"

"Well, Lieutenant O'Malley, I have to confess I haven't gone to church since I came to America, but I certainly will as soon as I can." "Sunday is a fine day to start, and I'd be happy to have you join me this Sunday, and you can go to church with me."

Shannon replied, "Thank you. I'll let you know on Friday if I can join you this Sunday."

"Just know, Ms. McGuire, it's a standing offer if you find it impossible to make it this Sunday."

When Shannon looked at Sean, all she could think of was what the nuns at school always told them: the only thing boys ever thought about was having sex with girls. Then she thought of the only thing she and her girl friends ever talked and thought about was having sex with boys and how not to get pregnant. Many of her friends had sex, got pregnant, left school, and got married, while some of her friends got pregnant, left school, and gave their babies up for adoption. As much as she was tempted, she and her beau had never had sex and decided to wait until after they were married.

So what happened when he got to America? He had sex with some Italian girl, gotten her pregnant, and married her. So when Shannon arrived in America to marry her love, she found she was left out in the cold with no husband and living on the streets.

Right now, Shannon needed to learn her job and stop thinking about Sean. She knew she would be working all day with her new boss, Indian Leader. She hoped she could remember all the things about working in an office. She thought she had done a good job working in the school office for four years, and it didn't take her long to learn everything about her job there.

Sean said, "Ms. McGuire, you seem to have gone far away from our conversation, so I'll say good day to you and see you tomorrow."

Shannon replied, "Sorry, Lieutenant O'Malley. I'm concerned about learning my new job."

"No worries, you'll do just fine. Just listen to what Captain Leader tells you. He is a very good teacher."

Sean walked away and Shannon thought, He's a handsome devil. I'm going to have to watch myself with him because I can tell he's a real temptation to me. I don't know anything about him at all. He may be married and have six kids for all I know.

Indian Leader arrived and said, "Good morning, Ms. McGuire, are you ready to get started to learn your responsibilities for taking care of the New York City Harbor Police Department office?"

"Yes, sir, I'm ready."

Captain Leader said, "Your primary responsibilities are to keep track of the personnel who work in this department. First, you will need to make a file for each person who works in the department. In this file, you should have all the information concerning their:

- Full name
- Citizenship
- Address
- Telephone number, if they have one
- Previous employers
- Married; single
- Rank
- Job description
- Salary

"Shannon, you can make your own form for this information. Then let me see it to either OK it or suggest changes. I hope you don't mind me calling you by your first name, but it saves time and we have a lot to do in a short time."

"No problem, sir. I know my name, and I don't consider it rude to just call me by my first name."

"Good, the next form you need to make is a daily report form for each person to sign in and out, so we know who came to work each day and the time they came in. The last form you will need to make will be the most important one to everyone who works here, and that is the report that goes to the payroll department, so everyone gets paid for working here. Oh, one other form you will need to make for me is a report sheet that each officer fills out every day, describing their activities for the day. This form needs to include such things as if they make an arrest; what the arrest was for; if they issued a warning to someone, which must include the citizen's name and address and why they were given a warning notice. Also, the area they patrolled for the day and a list of any complaint they heard from a citizen, what the complaint was, and what, if anything, the officer could do to correct the problem. Shannon, I think all this should keep you pretty busy for the rest of the day."

"Yes, sir. I think so. One question I have is, after I design these forms and you approve them, how do we get copies made of them?" "I'll have them taken to a printer to make up about three months' worth of forms at a time to see if we need to make any changes in them after we have time to check out how well they work for our people."

"Thank you, sir."

Shannon began designing and making the forms, and Indian was right, it took her almost all day to get them designed and laid out. When she was finished with them, she took them to Captain Leader's office to have him look them over. With the exception of the daily officer report form, he made no changes to any of the forms, and the only change he suggested on the daily officer report form was to give the officer more space to write their information in. Captain Leader said, "You've done a fine job on all these reports.

Just give the officers a little more room to write on the daily officer report form, and tomorrow, we'll go to the printer and order the forms. I think you will need to go with me because in the future, it will be your job to make sure we don't run out of any of the forms."

When Shannon finished work that day and made her way to their apartment, she was tired but very happy about her day.

She had only been home for a short time before Michael came in and asked, "So, my love, how did your first day at the new job go?" "It went well, and I certainly like all the people I work with, and my boss, Captain Leader, certainly knows how to let you learn your job."

"You sound like you really like him, Shannon."

"I certainly do. He knows what he wants done and then gets out of your way and lets you do it."

"Did you meet anyone else you think you really like, working there?"

"I did. His name is Lieutenant Sean O'Malley from Ireland, and he invited me to go to church with him on Sunday. He seems like a really nice young man.

Michael saw a twinkle in Shannon's eyes when she said Sean O'Malley's name and said, "You know what I think? You've already got a thing for Mr. O'Malley."

"Oh, Michael."

"You can say, oh, Michael, but I saw how your eyes twinkled when you said his name."

"Michael, we need to go have something for dinner." "Yes, we do."

10

WHAT ABOUT THE WEDDING

Patricia Sterling said to her children, Joan and Michael, "I don't know what we are going to do about your wedding, Joan. Joan, your father has been missing for more than six weeks, and no one has been able to find out anything about what has happened to him."

Michael said, "Robert's folks have been sitting around in the hotel, waiting all this time, not knowing what to do. I know they had planned to do some study with some of their professors at the university where they graduated to find out about any new tools they might be able to use in their teaching back in their Indian school, but I'm sure they can't do much more here."

Joan joined in and said, "I understand Indian and Rocky are now working to help establish a Harbor Police Department to help passengers to be safer when they are at the docks. Too bad, they didn't have such a police force in place before, then maybe Father wouldn't be missing. Which leaves Serene and Latesha with nothing to do but visit together and shop, which I'm sure they both must hate."

Patricia replied, "Joan, I doubt that they hate that, but I'm sure Latesha needs to get back to work with her father, and Serene wants to get back to her ranch in Texas. Therefore, I think we have to go ahead with your wedding either next week or the week after that. We will have to send out new invitations to let everyone know the new date. However, I guess before we can do that, we'll have to check to see if our church and our minister are available. Michael, you will have to fill in for your father. You'll have to walk your sister down the aisle and give her away. Joan, you have no idea how much your father wanted to be involved in your wedding."

"I know, Mother, he was certainly against me marrying Robert at first, but after he got to know him and work with him, he was one of Robert's biggest supporters."

Patricia called their minister and checked on the availability of the church and if their minister would be available to do the ceremony. She was told the next week wasn't possible because he already had a large wedding scheduled for that day. So the wedding would be on the following Saturday, in two weeks.

Next, Patricia telephoned the catering service and asked if they could do the reception on that Saturday and was told they couldn't. So Patricia decided they would have the reception at their home and have Chef Charles prepare the meal. So now, they only needed the printer to make the new wedding invitations and get them sent out to give their guests enough time to plan on attending Joan and Robert's wedding on June 30.

Joan was still going to be a June bride, like she had always planned to be; but instead of the first of the month, she would be married on the last day of the month. Joan needed to call Robert and tell him the wedding was on so he could make new plans for their honeymoon.

She had no idea of what he planned, but she was pretty sure he and her father had worked out the plans for their honeymoon. Wherever they would be going, she knew it would be wonderful because Robert was always so thoughtful.

Joan telephoned Robert to tell him they were going to go ahead with their wedding in two weeks, even without her father since no one had any idea of what happened to him. Robert seemed to be rather upset when Joan told him they had decided to go ahead with the wedding without her father.

Robert told Joan he knew her father had been looking forward to their wedding so much, he was sure if they went ahead with the wedding without him, he would never forgive them.

Joan assured him, "Robert, you know I told you that I can always get my way with Father. He'll forgive us if we can ever find him. Don't worry about him being mad at us."

Robert said, "I'm not worried about him being mad. I'm worried about how hurt he will be not to be part of our wedding. Joan, I think we should run another ad in the newspaper and increase the reward to a hundred thousand dollars for information helping to find your father and bring him safely home. Talk to your mother and Michael about what I said, about running new ads and offering an increased reward of a hundred thousand dollars for his safe return to his family."

"OK, Robert, I'll talk to Mother and Michael about it and see what they think."

Patricia and Michael both agreed with Robert about running new ads with the increased reward for Father's safe return to his family.

Michael said, "I'll take care of running the ads in the newspaper. Maybe the increased reward will help us turn up something about what's happened to Father."

The ads started running the next day and got a lot of attention in the dock area of New York City where Michael Sterling was last seen. It certainly caught the attention of one man named Don San Marco who began asking everyone in his gang of thieves if they remembered robbing this man a few weeks ago by the trolley stop. No one he talked with remembered robbing him.

Don San Marco told his men, "I want you to keep an eye out for this man. If we could find him, it would make us a lot of money."

Patricia telephoned the printing company, who had done the wedding invitation before for Joan and Robert's wedding, to have them made again with the same information, except for the new date for the wedding. She asked them if they could get the invitations printed and delivered to her as soon as possible. The printing company told her they would have them to her in the morning.

The following morning, around ten o'clock, the invitations were delivered, and as soon as Patricia had them in her hands, she gave them to her secretary, Mrs. Jones, and asked her to please get them in the mail that afternoon. Mrs. Jones told Mrs. Sterling she would have them ready to go out in time for the post that afternoon if she could have one of the maids help her.

Joan told Mrs. Jones, "I'll be glad to help you with the invitation. I'm sure I have more time than one of the maids."

Mrs. Jones replied, "Thank you. That would be very nice of you if you have the time, Ms. Joan."

"I don't have anything else going on today, and they are for my wedding. I think I could certainly help with my own invitations."

Mrs. Jones smiled and said, "We'd better get started right away to be able to get all these addressed and posted this afternoon."

Mrs. Jones and Joan went to Mrs. Jones's office and began addressing and putting stamps on each of the one hundred invitations. To begin with, each of them were writing the name and address of the people who were being sent an invitation, then placing the invitation card inside the envelope, then sealing the envelope and placing a stamp on it.

Joan suggested, "Perhaps we could do this faster if you addressed the envelope and then let me put them in the envelope, seal them up, and put on the stamp."

They tried doing it Joan's way, and it seemed like they were getting the invitations done much faster. After about an hour, Joan asked Mrs. Jones if she needed a break from doing all the addressing of the envelopes.

Mrs. Jones said, "Perhaps we should trade jobs for a while and let my writing hand have a rest. It's beginning to hurt a little bit."

After that, they changed jobs every hour, and after taking an hour break for a bit of lunch and a bathroom break, they were able to finish the invitations just before five o'clock that afternoon.

Joan said, "We did a good job getting all these invitations finished today. I had no idea how much work it was to send out one hundred invitations. I'm sorry I didn't help you with the first ones you sent out."

"I did have more time when I sent out the first ones for you, but it took me three days to do them all by myself."

"Thank you, Mrs. Jones. I appreciate all your hard work."

"I want to thank you, Ms. Joan, for helping me. It was fun having you help me."

"Mrs. Jones, I thought it was fun working with you too. I really enjoyed being with you today. I'll get one of the men to take the invitations to the post office, so we have them in today's mail, which means you can tell Mother you were able to get all the invitations out and in the post today."

Mrs. Jones gave Joan a big smile and replied, "I surely will, and I will tell her I couldn't have done it without you."

Joan beamed at what Mrs. Jones said. Then she rang for the butler, Charles, to have someone take the invitations to the post office.

Mrs. Jones met Mrs. Sterling as she was leaving for the night and said, "Mrs. Sterling, I want you to know that with Ms. Joan's help, the invitations have all been sent out."

Patricia replied, "That's wonderful, my dear. I'm glad Joan was some help to you."

Mrs. Jones said, "No, Mrs. Sterling, Ms. Joan was a major help in getting the invitations out today."

Patricia then smiled and said, "Thank you, Mrs. Jones. It's nice to hear one of the Sterlings was able to be a big help to someone. Good night, Mrs. Jones."

11

BACK WORKING THE DOCKS

Don San Marco called all his gang of thieves together for a meeting to outline a new plan to start working the docks again. He began the meeting by telling his men income had dropped to half what it used to be before the Harbor Police.

Don San Marco said, "I studied how patrol area. We can work area follow one simple rule. Patrol routes only have two officers walk route.

Officers, always walk same direction on route. All we do wait officers pass by. When no see officers, we make move, take whatever want from people.

Other thing, I do. Make life tougher on police officers. We knock off few them. Send message Irish men, not good, mess Mafia, they messing with big boys. I want you men look better. Get cleaned up, not just buy booze and broads. Get clothes, look like you somebody. I tired look you mugs, like bunch bums, without nickel to name. You Don San Marco men, not just guy who take money from suckers. I got big plans, we move up town, take over all hookers in Manhattan and all the gambling. Anybody gets in way, fish food. Anybody runs hookers, operates gambling, comes us or he out of business. He need no business, people swimming with fish need nothing. OK, schools over, hit streets. Make Don San Marco happy man, bring home loot."

Don San Marco said, "Charlie, Louie, you come me. It time we rid couple Irish cops."

The three men walked directly to the harbor, and as soon as they got there, they met two of the Harbor police officers.

Don San Marco said, "So how go today, officers?"

One of the officers replied, "Everything's pretty quiet around here."

The three men passed by the two officers, and after they were about ten feet behind them, the three men turned around and began firing their weapons, and the officers fell dead.

Don San Marco, Charlie, and Louie put away their weapons and began running and shouting," Somebody shot two police officers." The three of them hadn't gone far when they met two officers, and Don San Marco said, "Officers, men shot two policemen, run off other direction. I think officers need help."

With that, the two officers ran down the sidewalk, looking for the two downed officers, and when they arrived there, they found two officers lying on the sidewalk. They found both of the officers were dead. One of the officers began blowing his whistle, and several other police officers soon arrived at the scene. One of the officers was sent to the police station to get in touch with either Chief Stone or Captain Leader.

Chief Stone was working in his office when an officer came running into the police station, screaming, "We've got two officers shot."

Chief Stone ran to the front of the station and said, "Officer Kelly, take me to where the officers that have been shot are."

"Yes, sir."

Officer Kelly went out the door of the police station with Chief Stone following right behind him. When they got to the scene of the shooting, Rocky could see the men had been turned over onto their backs to check to see if they were alive.

Rocky asked, "Which of you officers were at the scene first?"

Officer Toomey said, "Officer Spring and I were the first ones here, sir."

"Tell me what you saw, Officer Toomey."

"When we arrived, I saw both of the officers lying face down on the sidewalk. They had been shot in the back."

"What did you do next, Officer Toomey?"

"We both blew our whistles as a signal that officers needed help. Then I sent Officer Spring to the station to get either you or Captain Leader to come to the scene, sir."

"Then what did you do?"

"I turned the officers over to see if they were still alive. They weren't." "Did you see anyone else in the area when you got here?"

"No, sir, the only people we saw after we heard the shots was when we were coming to see what happened. We met three men who were screaming that two officers had been shot, and the men who shot them were running away in the opposite direction from them." "Officer Toomey and Officer Spring, tell me what these three men that you met looked like?"

Officer Spring said, "Well, we didn't get a very go look at them since they were running away from the direction we were going. As Officer Toomey said, there were three men. One of the men wasn't very tall or very big, but he was the one who was yelling and he was very well dressed. He had kind of a dark complexion, like maybe he was Italian. He had very shiny black hair, and his hair was really slicked down. The other two men looked like they were, well, like some of the bums who hang around the docks all the time. Both of them were medium build, not too tall, but a lot taller than the one guy."

"Gentlemen, I'm afraid those were the killers you met."

Rocky continued talking, "I think we have just been delivered a message from Don San Marco. He's the gangster who ran all the crime around the docks until you men started patrolling the area.

I'm afraid this won't be the last attack he and his men are going to be committing against us. We need to get the bodies of our fallen officers taken care of and notify their families. The job of notifying their families will be handled by Captain Leader and myself."

The bodies of the two officers were taken to a funeral home, and Chief Stone told the funeral home the department would be responsible for paying for their funerals. By the time Rocky returned to the police station, Indian had returned from picking up some office supplies for Shannon.

Rocky told Indian what happened, but Indian had already heard the news of their two officers being gunned down. It was already all over the station.

Captain Leader asked Shannon to please give him the addresses of the two slain officers.

After Indian had the addresses, he and Rocky went to both of the homes of the officers to inform their families of the deaths of their loved ones. Both families took the news like, in their lives, the loss of a loved one was nothing new. These people had lived through so much adversity, and having a family member die was like it happened every day.

The city coroner recovered the bullets from the police officers' bodies and gave them to Chief Stone as evidence of the crime. Rocky and Indian could see the men were each shot at least four times and by two different caliber guns. One of the guns had a smaller-sized caliber bullet than the other two.

Rocky said, "These six bullets came from .38-caliber guns. These other two bullets are smaller, but I have no idea what kind of a gun they came from."

Their police officers were all armed with .38-caliber guns, but both Rocky and Indian continued to carry their own guns, .44-caliber Colts. If Don San Marco thought killing two Irish cops would scare away the other Irish officers, he was sadly mistaken. It melded the men in the department into one unit, dedicated to finding their killers and punishing them.

Even the six Italians bonded into the unit; if they had been outsiders before, now they were part of the team. They were no longer from Ireland and Italy; they were New York City Harbor police officers, just Americans.

A joint funeral was planned for the slain police officers three days later, at St. John's Catholic Church, where both men were members.

Chief Stone issued an order that except for eight officers who would be working the dock area the day of the funeral, all officers of the Harbor Police Department would attend the funeral in full dress uniform. They would march together from the Harbor Police Station with Chief Stone and Captain Leader at the head of the company, followed by Lieutenant O'Malley and the members of the honor guard. Then, all the rest of the officers would walk, five abreast, to the church. There, the officers would have their own seating section in the church.

When the funeral service was over, the Harbor Police Department officers would be the first people dismissed from the services, with twelve of the officers serving as pallbearers going to the two caskets, with Lieutenant O'Malley and the seven officers in the honor guard stationed in front of the caskets.

Chief Stone and Captain Leader would lead the rest of the officers out of the church and form up the company to wait for the honor guard and the caskets to be placed onto special funeral wagons. Once the congregation was dismissed and the family came out of the church, Chief Stone and Captain Leader would lead the officers and the rest of the procession from the church to the cemetery.

Two days before, the Chief of Police of New York City, William Thompson, telephoned Rocky and asked if it would be OK if he had his officers taking care of the traffic from the church to the cemetery. Rocky told Chief Thompson that it would be greatly appreciated. The two chiefs decided it was very important for them to meet soon to be able to have their departments working together.

After the final prayers were said for the two slain officers, Lieutenant O'Malley's honor guard fired a twenty-one gun salute to the officers. In the background, as the flags were being presented to the families by Lieutenant O'Malley, a bagpipe was playing softly off in the distance. Chief Thompson had sent his bagpipe player to play for the end of the services at the cemetery without telling Rocky he planned to do it. Rocky thought that was a class act shown by the New York City Chief of Police. Then everything was completed with the services.

Rocky and Indian said their thanks for the service the two officers gave to the department to their families. Then they marched the officers back to the Harbor Police Station. As they were marching back to the police station, Indian saw his wife, Serene, and Rocky's wife, Latesha, standing by the corner of the entrance to the dock area. Indian also saw that two of Latesha's father's security officers were with them to be certain that they were not kidnapped or harmed while they were in the dock area. After they marched past their wives, Indian asked Rocky if he knew they were coming to the funeral. He didn't nor did Indian know his wife was coming.

When they arrived back at the police station, they found two of their officers had arrested two men they caught in the act of robbing two passengers who had just arrived in New York. The arriving passengers were grateful that the Harbor Police were on duty and had caught the two thieves before they got away with all their money and their other valuables.

After Rocky and Indian questioned the two men, they wouldn't say if they worked for anyone, but when Don San Marco's name was mentioned, both Rocky and Indian knew they were two of his men, just by the look in their eyes.

What they saw in the men's eyes was fear, just knowing they had been caught by the Harbor Police, and they had no idea of what Don San Marco would do to them for being caught.

12

DINNER WITH HENRY HUDSON IV

Rocky had asked Indian and Serene to come to dinner at his father-in-law's home, Henry Hudson IV, that evening, where he and his wife, Latesha, also lived.

Indian had a message waiting for him when he returned from the funeral of their two fallen police officers. The message read, "Please come home with Rocky tonight since I am already at Latesha's. Love, Serene."

Indian said, "Rocky, I guess I'll be going home with you when we're finished working tonight since I have a message that Serene is already at your house. You remember, I told you Serene and Latesha were at the funeral. I saw them as we were coming into the dock area." Rocky replied, "Man, I can't get rid of you now that I'm working with you every day. I know you and Serene were invited to dinner tonight, but I thought I'd at least get a couple of hours away from you when I got home from work before you came to dinner.

Now you're telling me you are going straight home with me." Indian laughed and said, "Don't blame me. It's our wives.

They're together every minute. When I go to work, but before I get out the door of the hotel, Latesha is there to pick Serene up to go, well, only God knows where they go."

Rocky replied, "You're right. You people need to go back to Texas so Latesha can go back to working with her father, changing the world with all their new inventions for the twentieth century."

Indian said, "Sometime, when we're not so busy saving passengers come in and out of the docks of New York City, along with looking out for the people who work here. I would love for you to tell me about some of these new inventions. By the way, Rocky, how in the hell did we get mixed up starting a Harbor Police Department in the first place and getting ourselves into this mess? How come a couple of cowboys are trying to help out these big city folks? Why didn't we keep our noses out of their business?"

Rocky replied, "I don't know, but I think they think we are some kind of white knights who just rode into town to save their city."

Indian said, "Whoa, I'm beginning to wonder if we're going to be able to save our own necks, getting involved in this business. I've heard some of those Italians boys are pretty tough. Rocky, I guess we can't just do it like we did in the old days. We'd just find that Don San Marco and shoot him down and get it over with."

"I guess we can't, Indian, but it sounds like the quickest way to solve most of the crime around the docks: just find him and send him to hell. Indian, is there anything else you need to do before we head out of here for the night?"

"No, partner, I think we've done about all we can do today. We gave our two dead officers a good send-off, and I'm sure we sent a message to Don San Marco that the Harbor Police Force is united. On top of that, two of our officers arrested a couple of his men while we were at the funerals.

Let's get out of here, Rocky."

Rocky and Indian signed out for the day and took a trolley to Rocky's home. When they arrived and walked inside the house, their wives were waiting to welcome them with a kiss. Latesha and Serene both told them how proud they were of the way they organized their fallen officers' funerals and said they both looked so handsome leading their officers in the march to and from the cemetery. After listening to their wives' praises and enjoying it completely, Latesha suggested they join her father in the library for a drink before dinner.

When they went into the library, Latesha introduced Indian to her father, and he, in turn, introduced Indian to his chief of security, Colonel Chuck Carson. Henry asked Indian and Rocky what they would like to drink, and both replied, "Whiskey."

Henry poured both the men a small glass of whiskey and said, "Rocky, Indian, I've asked Chuck to come and join us for dinner, so he can give you some information on this man, Don San Marco. Rocky, why don't you and Indian sit down and listen to what Chuck has to say about this man?"

Rocky and Indian sat down on couches with their wives sitting next to them.

Chuck began by saying, "Henry, tells me you have both met Don San Marco. You probably weren't too impressed with him when you met him due to his slight size and his fancy manner of dressing. However, he's a lot more than what meets the eye. Gentlemen, Don San Marco came from Sicily, and he's part of a huge organization of crime bosses headed by one man living in Sicily. In the first place when you hear Don San Marco, you think his first name is Don. It's not, his first name is Joseph. Don is a title, and in their organization, San Marco is called a godfather. The name of the overall organization from Sicily is called the Mafia.

"In New York City, they have five dons, one for each of the five boroughs. The don of Manhattan is the kingpin of New York City because he's the one who sends the most money back to Sicily. Don't underestimate the power of these men. They have politicians, police officers, and judges on their payroll. They have a code: get in their way, they kill you or they have you killed. Killing two of your Harbor police officers was just a way to let you know, keep out of their way or, next time, it could be you. I've spoken to the US attorney general about Don San Marco, and he told me Don San Marco is the son of Don Giovanni, the head of the Mafia in Sicily. "From the information the attorney general has, his father sent Don San Marco to become the head of America's Mafia. His first job was to take over the Manhattan operation, which included his disposing of the old don, who was found skimming money from what was supposed to be sent to Sicily. Don San Marco arrived in New York one day, and the old don was found shot to death in an alleyway off Broadway the following day. The police found he had been killed with a small-caliber gun unlike anything they had ever seen before. Right now, the attorney general says Don San Marco's men are taking over all the prostitutes and gambling operations in Manhattan. Anyone who isn't willing to join with Don San Marco is simply killed.

"However, since the word is out, the numbers of dead pimps and gamblers have dropped a lot over the past few days. It appears it's better to share than die. Now you know what you're up against battling Don San Marco and his men. The attorney general says Don San Marco's organization has grown three times larger than it was a month ago. He has more men than you and the New York City Police Department in Manhattan put together and has a weapon you don't have, the willingness to kill anyone who opposes him."

Indian asked, "How does the attorney general have so much information about Don San Marco?"

"Because one of San Marco's lieutenants works for the attorney general, but he is limited as to what he has been able to prove that would have any chance of getting San Marco sent to prison or hanging him. If his man makes the wrong move, he can wind up as dead as the people who oppose San Marco. Fear is a wonderful weapon. The fear of losing one's life works very well for Don San Marco and the Mafia. When they show they are so ready and willing to kill, it makes getting their way much easier."

Henry broke in and said, "The butler tells me dinner is ready to be served, if after hearing all this, any of you still has an appetite."

Rocky replied, "I think we better eat. It might be Indian's and my last meal."

Indian said, "I certainly don't want to miss my last meal."

Then, Rocky and Indian both started laughing. However, their wives didn't think it was very funny nor did their host.

Indian said, "If you had any idea of the number of people who wanted and have tried to kill me who failed, you would understand why Rocky and I are laughing. Maybe the Mafia can kill us, but if I was them, I wouldn't place a big bet on it. Rocky and I know we could die any day just like anyone else, but because we have put our life on the line every day for so many years, it's kind of hard to scare us. However, Colonel Carson, don't misunderstand my attempt to bring a little humor to what you have told us.

Please don't think it isn't appreciated, it is greatly appreciated. You have given us an insight into how this Mafia operates, and it will certainly help us in trying to deal with them. On behalf of Rocky and myself, I do really want to thank you."

Rocky added, "We had no idea how big an organization we were up against, and I agree with Indian. It will be a great help to us trying to combat them."

Latesha said, "It's time we relaxed a little and tried to enjoy the evening and the dinner our folks have prepared for us. I know it will certainly be welcomed."

Henry took his place at the head of the table, and Latesha was seated to the right of Henry, Rocky was on his left, and Serene was seated next to Rocky. Indian was seated next to Latesha, and Colonel Carson was seated next to him. Latesha's announcement that the staff had prepared a wonderful dinner for them was absolutely correct; their dinner was fabulous. After dinner, Indian and Serene were taken by the Henry's coachman to the Waldorf Astoria Hotel, where they had been living since they arrived in New York.

Serene asked, "Indian, you know Joan and Robert's wedding is coming up in less than two weeks. How much longer are you planning on staying to help Rocky with the Harbor police?"

"I don't have any idea. I don't think we can leave right after their wedding because Rocky is going to need help getting the police force more experienced before I leave him by himself. I will have to say that Lieutenant Sean O'Malley is doing a good job because of his experience as a captain in the police department in Dublin, Ireland. We're lucky to have him, and I'm sure at some point, he can take over as the chief of the department when Rocky decides to leave."

"Indian, we can't stay too long. We've got a ranch to run in Texas, and if you're going to be needed here for some time, I will have to go back to Texas by myself."

"Serene, my love, don't make a decision too quickly. Let me see how things are going for a little while after the wedding. I don't want to not be with you. I love you too much to be away from you for very long."

13

BATTLE WITH THE MAFIA

The following morning, when Rocky and Indian arrived at the Harbor Police Station, they found Lieutenant Sean O'Malley busy writing up a report on a gun battle with two of their officers and at least two men.

Lieutenant O'Malley said, "I was making rounds, checking on how everyone was doing early this morning when I heard gunfire and rushed to see what was happening. When I arrived, I found two of our officers taking fire from two or more shooters hiding in some trees. I could see Officer O'Rourke was wounded, and Officer McQueen was trying to look after him and, at the same time, return fire at two or more shooters. From my position, I found I was behind the men shooting at our officers and managed to get off rounds, killing one of the shooters and wounding a second man.

"The second man continued to shoot back at me as he was trying to get away, but I fired back and killed him too. If there was a third man involved, he fled the scene without firing a shot at me. Both Officer O'Rourke and Officer McQueen say there was a third shooter, however, if there was, perhaps he saw me when I arrived at the scene and left because he could see I was behind them."

Rocky said, "Great job, Sean. How is Officer O'Rourke? How bad is his wound?"

"When they took him to the hospital, he was doing fair. He was hit in the right side, but they seemed to have been able to stop the bleeding by the time I left there."

Indian said, "That's good that they were able to stop the bleeding. I'll go to the hospital to check on Officer O'Rourke while Chief Stone goes over the reports and checks on the two men who were killed. I'm sure we have a very good idea of who sent these men. Chief Stone, I'll go check on Officer O'Rourke's condition and be back as soon as I can. If O'Rourke is up to it, I'll get a report from him on the shooting."

Rocky replied, "Thanks, Captain Leader. Tell O'Rourke he'll be in our prayers, and I'll be up to see him as soon as I can."

When Indian arrived at the hospital, he found Officer O'Rourke was in worse condition then they thought, and his wife and priest were with him.

When Indian asked Mrs. O'Rourke how her husband was doing, she told Indian he died ten minutes ago.

Indian said, "I'm so sorry to hear about your husband. He was a very good man and a fine officer. I can assure you his killers will be punished.

Again, I'm so sorry. If there is anything we can do, please let us know.

You know, we will take care of all his funeral costs and work something out to help you and your children. I believe you have a boy and a girl, don't you?"

"Yes, we do."

"How old are they?"

"My son is eleven, and my daughter is fourteen. I don't know how we're going to make it without Timothy. He loved his job more than anything he had ever done."

"Mrs. O'Rourke, I'm sure the department will be able to come up with some way to help you."

The priest said, "Laura, you know the church will help you too." Then the priest said, "Captain Leader, I'm Father Murphy, and I would like to offer my services to your department. I know most of your officers belong to my parish. I feel some of your young men are going to need some counseling after losing Timothy in the line of duty."

Indian replied, "I think that's a very good idea, Father Murphy. We would be grateful to have you talk with all our officers. You understand, we work three shifts, so you would need to come to the station at least three times to be able to meet with all our officers. I would say it would be better if it was after Timothy's funeral, if you think that would be OK."

"Captain Leader, I do think it would be better timing to meet with your officers after the funeral."

"Thank you, Father Murphy." Indian then said, "Mrs. O'Rourke, I'm so sorry about Timothy. I will be talking to you later."

"Thank you, Captain Leader. I appreciate you coming to check on Timothy."

Indian turned and left Mrs. O'Rourke and Father Murphy as they continued to pray over Timothy.

By the time Indian returned to the Harbor Police Department, he had made up his mind what he was going to do, but he had no plans on telling anyone at the department, especially Rocky or Serene. As soon as Indian walked into the police station, everyone was asking how Officer O'Rourke was doing, and when he told them he had died, a hush fell over the station.

Indian met with Rocky and Lieutenant Sean O'Malley in Rocky's office, and when they heard Officer O'Rourke had died, Sean couldn't believe it.

He was certain Officer O'Rourke would have been all right. Sean was heartbroken about losing an officer on his watch.

Indian and Rocky told him it wasn't his fault because he didn't fire the shots that killed Officer O'Rourke. Both Indian and Rocky told Sean they had lost men on their watch while serving as law enforcement officers.

It didn't make Sean feel any better, but he at least he understood he wasn't the only one to lose someone working under him.

Sean never had this kind of problems when he was a captain with the Dublin Police Department. They didn't have so many bad guys running around with guns. His men there got hurt breaking up fights in the pubs, and then the guys that were fighting would quit fighting each other and began fighting the police officers instead. Sean thought about what a country Ireland was and what a different country America was. Here, the bad guys played for keeps, which meant the police officers were going to have to react the same way. Three days later, the funeral for Officer O'Rourke was held, and again, the department's officers marched to the cemetery with Chief Stone and Captain Leader leading the procession, the same as it had been done for the two officers who had been killed earlier. Father Murphy kept his word and came and talked with all the officers on all three of their shifts. Indian told Rocky that he was going to work the second shift for a while to see if he could help the officers since Rocky was working with the day shift and Lieutenant O'Malley was with the third shift. Indian decided that to solve the killing of their police officers, they would have to get rid of the Mafia boss man, Don San Marco, and he planned to do exactly that. He didn't know how he was going to do it yet, but he planned to find a way.

Serene was not happy with Indian working the second shift, but she knew he felt he had to help his men out. The third evening he was working, he wasn't dressed in his uniform but in his western clothes and was walking about ten minutes behind one of the police patrols when he came upon a robbery in progress. Indian saw the two men as they were robbing an elderly couple who had just arrived in New York. The two robbers were so involved with making sure they had all the old couple's valuables, they didn't see Indian slip up behind them, and he told them to put their hands up in the air. The two men did as they were told. Then Indian told them to back away from the couple. Again, they did as they were told. Indian told the couple to pick up all their things and go to the police station. He told them how to get there while all the time, keeping his eyes on the two robbers. Indian used his police whistle to summon other police officers on patrol in the harbor area to come to his location. When two officers arrived, they saw Indian had captured two robbers. He told his officers to pick up the robbers' weapons and then to handcuff them. Next, he told his two officers to take the biggest man with them and lock him up. The officers asked Captain Leader what he was going to do with the other man. Indian said he wanted to have a talk with him by himself before bringing him to jail.

The two officers left with the one man, and then Indian said, "What's your name?"

The man said nothing, so Indian asked again, "I said, what's your name?"

The man again said nothing, so Indian took the man's arms, which were handcuffed behind his back, and began walking him into the trees and away from the walkway.

When they got into the trees, Indian pushed the man down on the ground and said, "This will be the last time you have a chance to tell me your name, because if I don't hear a name from you, the next sound you will hear is a gunshot. So what's your name?"

Indian pointed his six-gun directly at the man's head and cocked the hammer.

"It's Joseph San Marco."

Indian eased back the hammer on his Colt and asked, "You work for Don San Marco, don't you?"

"I don't know who that is."

Indian cocked the hammer on his Colt again and said, "I don't think you understood what I asked you. I asked if you work for Don San Marco."

Then Indian placed the barrel of his Colt directly on San Marco's forehead.

De Marco replied, "Yes, I work for him."

Indian asked, "Are you related to him? His name is San Marco and yours is San Marco?"

"No, San Marco isn't his real family's name. It's Giovanni." "Then why is he using the name San Marco?"

"Because he couldn't get a passport or a visa to come to America using his real name, so they paid off people in the government and got him and his family all new birth certificates and passports."

Indian said, "OK, so you're not his relative?" "No, I only work for him."

Indian pulled the Colt's barrel back from the man's head and said, "If you want to keep living, you're going to tell me where he lives, and then we're going to go see him, all right?"

"Whatever you say."

"Good, if you stand up, I'll take the handcuffs off and then we'll go see Don San Marco."

Indian pulled De Marco up from the ground, turned him around, and took off his handcuffs.

Indian said, "Now, we are going to walk over to Don San Marco's home so I can have a talk with him. You see, he is responsible for killing three of my police officers, and I don't like it. So I'm going to ask him to please stop killing them."

San Marco didn't say anything; he just rubbed his wrist where the handcuffs had been fastened. He led Indian directly to Don San Marco's house and said, "That's his place, across the street, but you know he has several bodyguards looking after him. You're surely not stupid enough to go in there by yourself, are you?"

"No, sir, I'm not going in there by myself. You're going with me."

"Man, you're crazy. They'll kill both of us before we get inside the door."

"Then I guess you'd better help get me in without us getting killed."

"How do you think I'm going to do that?"

"You're going to tell them your partner and you were captured by the police and I came along and killed the two police officers and freed you, but your partner was killed during the gun battle."

"Do you think they will believe me?"

"They better because you're going to be in front of me."

De Marco and Indian walked up to the house, and two men stepped out of the shadows and asked, "Who's with you? Where's Charlie?"

De Marco said, "Charlie's dead, and this guy killed the two police officers who captured us, and we just got away before four more cops came running up. We need to see the boss."

The two guys got out of the way, and De Marco opened the door and walked inside the house with Indian right behind him. When they got inside the house, De Marco shouted "Watch out, this guy's a cop."

Before Indian could do anything, Don San Marco fired a shot, and De Marco fell to the floor at the same time Indian hit the floor. He quickly got back to his feet and saw Don San Marco with a gun. Indian fired two quick shots, and two bullets hit Don San Marco, one in the head and one in his chest.

The two bodyguards came rushing in, but Indian turned in time to fire two more shots, and the first man fell to the floor; as the other man tried to get back away from the door, Indian shot him twice. Indian looked around the house, but there was no one else there.

Indian checked the men over and found they were all dead, and when he checked Don San Marco's gun, he found it was a small- caliber gun unlike any gun he had ever seen before. Indian closed the door of the house and walked away as quickly as he could. When Indian returned to the police station, he asked where the man he captured was and was told he tried to make a run for it and they had to kill him.

Indian said to the two officers, "I'm sorry to hear that. The fellow I asked you to leave with me, I took off his handcuffs to talk to him, and he did the same thing—he ran off. I know I hit him at least once, but I couldn't find him in the dark. I'm sure he was hurt pretty bad, so I don't think he will bother us again."

Indian went into Rocky's office, took off his badge, put it on Rocky's desk along with a note he wrote, saying after Robert and Joan's wedding, he and Serene had to go back home to Texas. The note said they had too much to do at home and he just couldn't stay any longer, but he thought that the worst of the problems with the Mafia might be over.

14

HEADLINE IN THE MORNING NEWS

The next morning, Rocky picked up his morning paper before leaving to go to work at the New York City Harbor Police Department, and the headline screamed, "Mafia Boss and Three of His Men Found Dead."

The story continued. The New York City Police Department said they believed that a rival gang was responsible for the deaths because since Don San Marco had come to America, he and his Mafia gang had been muscling in on all the other gangs' territories in New York City. The newspaper story also said that a gun found near Don San Marco was linked to the death of a New York Harbor police officer.

Rocky shouted to Latesha, "Honey, have you seen the newspaper this morning?"

"No, I've been busy trying to get ready, so I can meet Serene. We're going shopping for something to wear for Joan's wedding."

"Latesha, you're never going to believe it, but someone killed the head of the Mafia and three of his men, and we know he was the one responsible for killing our police officers."

"Good, I'm glad someone did."

Rocky said, "I wonder if Indian has seen this story yet. I'm going to call him and see if he's seen the paper. I know he's going to be happy to hear what the paper said."

Rocky called the Waldorf Astoria and asked to be connected to Indian's room. Rocky could hear the phone ringing in Indian's room, and a few seconds later, Indian answered the phone.

After Indian said hello, Rocky said, "Indian, have you seen the paper this morning?"

"No, I haven't."

"Well, you're never going to believe it, but somebody killed Don San Marco last night and three of his men. The story in the paper says the police think one of the rival gangs he pushed out killed him. What do you think about that, Indian?"

"I think it's great. We caught two of his men last night, one of them I'd asked two of our officers to take to jail, but he tried to run and they had to shoot him and he died. The other guy, I kept myself to try to get some information from him before we locked him up. I took off his handcuffs and he ran off, but not before I shot him, but I lost him in the dark, but I'm pretty sure he was hit bad, maybe they'll find him somewhere around the docks today. Also, I need to tell you I put my badge on your desk and left you a note telling you Serene and I have to go home after Robert and Joan's wedding. We just can't stay any longer. You know we have a big ranch in Texas to run. Partner, I'm really sorry to run out on you, but we've got to get back to the ranch."

"I certainly understand it, Indian. I just want you to know how much I appreciate everything you did helping me organizing and starting the Harbor Police Department. I could never have done it by myself. I'm sure going to miss you, my friend."

"You know, Rocky, I'm going to miss you too. I really enjoyed working with you, but I'm pretty sure you could have handled starting the Harbor Police Department by yourself, but I know it wouldn't have been as much fun without me."

Rocky laughed and said, "Damn right, Indian, it was fun working with you, and you made it a lot easier on me starting the Harbor Police Department."

Indian replied, "Rocky, the only thing we didn't get accomplished was that we didn't find Mr. Sterling. I'm sure sorry about that."

"Well, Indian, I guess we can't win them all."

"I tell you, Rocky. I'm not used to losing, I feel like we lost that one."
"Indian, maybe he'll turn up before the wedding yet. Maybe our luck
is turning. With someone killing Don San Marco, who knows, maybe
our department will find him."

"That would be great. Say, Rocky, aren't you going to be late
for work?"

"Talking with you, I forgot. You're right. I've got to go."

Rocky hung up the telephone and was soon on his way to his office.

When he arrived at his office, he found Indian's badge and his note,
and after reading Indian's note, Rocky said out loud to no one, "I know
Indian killed Don San Marco and his men last night. Indian said he
didn't like losing, so he made sure he didn't lose to San Marco. I'll be
damned. I can't believe he did that without telling me he did." A few
minutes later, Shannon came into Rocky's office and asked him if he
needed anything special for her to do today for him. Rocky told her he
did; he needed her to write up and post a notice on the bulletin board
that effective today, Captain Indian Leader was leaving the department
to return to his ranch in Texas and Lieutenant Sean O'Malley was
hereby promoted to captain.

Shannon said, "I'm sorry to hear about Captain Leader leaving us.
He was a great man to work with. I'm certainly going to miss him."
Rocky replied, "Well, Ms. Shannon, not nearly as much as I will be
missing him. He knew everything about operating a police department
in a big city by working in St. Louis as a deputy sheriff.

I'm really going to miss him."

"Well, Chief Stone, all of us are going to be missing him. The
department will just never be the same without him."

"Shannon, we'll just have to find a way to keep doing our jobs."
"Yes, sir, so I better get busy."

Shannon left to make up the notice to post on the bulletin board,
and Rocky went to find Sean O'Malley. Rocky found Sean and asked
him to come into his office. When they got into Rocky's office, Rocky
asked Sean to sit down, and he proceeded to tell Sean that Captain
Leader was leaving to go back home to Texas, and he was promoting

him to captain to replace him. Then Rocky asked Sean if he had anyone yet he thought they could promote to take his place.

Sean replied, "I think the best officer I've worked with so far is Officer Timothy Toomey. He learns quickly and has a better understanding of working in America, probably because he has been in America longer than any of the other men we have working here."

"Let's get him in here and talk with him."

"He's not here. He works on the three to eleven shift."

"OK, could you come back about three and we'll talk with him then?"

"Yes, sir."

"OK Sean, you go home and get some rest, and I'll see you around three this afternoon."

"OK, Chief. I'll see you this afternoon."

After Shannon finished making up the announcement to post on the bulletin board, she showed it to Chief Stone who approved it to post as she had written it. When Shannon returned to her desk she saw a copy of the missing person report about the missing rich man named John Sterling.

She laid the report down on her desk and then she picked it up again and studied the picture of John Sterling on the report. Shannon put the missing person report back down on her desk, then picked it up again and said to herself, "My god, that's Michael Gilley. No, it couldn't be, or could it?"

Shannon kept stewing about it and finally decided to go talk with Chief Stone about her thoughts. Shannon walked back to Chief Stone's office, found he wasn't there, so she went to the front desk and asked where Chief Stone was. She was told he had to go to a meeting with the port director and wouldn't be back until just before three this afternoon, and then he had a meeting with Captain O'Malley. Shannon returned to her desk to get back to her normal work, and it kept her busy the rest of the day until she left work to return to her apartment.

Michael wasn't scheduled to be home until sometime after five that afternoon, so Shannon thought she might walk over to Bob's Place to wait for him to get off work. She didn't arrive at Bob's Place until it was a little after five, and she saw Michael walking down the other side of the street and he hadn't seen her. When she got to the crosswalk, she made her way across the street to be on the same side of the street as Michael, and she hurried to catch up with him.

When she got up behind Michael, she said, "John Sterling."

Michael stopped and turned around and said, "Yes, may I help you?" Shannon looked at Michael and asked, "Are you John Sterling?" "Yes, I am. Shannon, I'm John Sterling. How did you know my name?"

"John, there are posters and missing persons notices everywhere, and I saw one on my desk at the police department this morning and thought the picture looked like you, my Michael Gilley. I can't believe it. You are John Sterling."

"Oh, Shannon, my wife and kids must be worried out of their minds about me."

"Michael, I mean, John, I'm sure they are. They are offering a reward of $100,000 for finding you and getting you safely back with your family."

"Shannon, my girl, I guess you just made yourself $100,000." "John, you didn't really know who you were, did you?"

"No, I had no idea until you called me by my name. Oh my god, my daughter Joan was supposed to be getting married a long time ago. Shannon, I have to go home and try to explain to my family what happened to me.

Shannon, you have to come with me, you saved my life and you have to come and live with me as part of my family. I love you, you know."

"I love you too, John, but I don't think your family is going to be happy having some strange girl from Ireland moving in with them." "Just wait, Shannon. You'll see, they will welcome you into our family."

"OK, John, I will go with you to your home, but I'll wait to see what your wife and kids have to say about me moving in with them."

John took Shannon's hand and led her to a coach and told the driver they wanted to go to 100 Park Avenue.

The coachman thought, These two must work in the mansion that's located at that address.

When they arrived at 100 Park Avenue, John gave the coachman all the money he had to pay for their trip. As the coachman drove away, he thought the people who owned the house must pay pretty well because it was the biggest tip he got all day.

John rang the doorbell and the butler, Claude, soon answered the door. When the butler saw these two people standing at the front door, he asked whom they would like to see.

John said, "Claude, it's me, John Sterling."

The butler misunderstood what he said and replied, "I'm sorry, sir, but Mr. John Sterling is not at home at this time."

Shannon looked at John puzzled and wondered if she made a mistake and that Michael wasn't John Sterling after all.

John said, "Claude, I'm John Sterling. You just don't recognize me with this beard."

Claude looked carefully at John and said, "Sir, it is you. I'm so happy to see that you are all right."

"Thank you, Claude. Would you take us to the library and find all my family and ask them to come there, so I can introduce them to my friend, Ms. Shannon McGuire."

"Yes, sir."

Claude turned and took them to the library and left them to find all of Mr. Sterling's family.

Patricia was the first of the family to arrive, and she flew directly into John's arms and said through her tears, "Oh, John, I've been so worried about you and been praying for your safe return."

John kissed her and held her closely as he could. Next, his daughter, Joan, came into the library, and she ran to him as soon as she saw him, and John reached out and took her in his arms. Now he had Patricia in his right arm and Joan in his left arm. Then his son, Michael, came into the library, and he too ran directly to his father who greeted him and then the four of them were holding each other in a big circle hug.

After a lot of tears and words of thanks for John's return home, John said, "Everyone, I want you to meet Ms. Shannon McGuire. She saved my life and took care of me since I've been gone. She found me in an alley with my head busted open and helped me to get up, and I have been living with her ever since. Until today, I had no idea of who I was. Shannon has been working for the New York City Harbor Police Department, and she saw a missing person notice with my picture on it today and figured out who I was. Then as I was walking down the street on the way to our home, she came up behind me and said my name: John Sterling. Then suddenly, I remembered who I was. Shannon, this is my wife, Patricia; daughter, Joan; and my son, Michael."

They each gave Shannon a hug and thanked her for looking after husband and father.

John said, "I want you all to know when Shannon found me, she was living in a box on fisherman's dock. We lived in that box for a long time and lived by eating food out of trash cans behind the restaurants. We found a way to make some money and were finally able to move into a small two-room apartment with a bathroom we had to share with two other families. Shannon came to America from Shannon, Ireland, to get married, but when she got here, the man she was going to marry had already married someone else. So we are the only family she has in America, and I've asked her to live with us, but she said she would only agree to do that if my family agreed to it too. However, she has no idea of what kind of family she might be getting herself into by moving in with the Sterlings." Patricia spoke first, "Shannon, I don't know you at all, but what I do know is if you got my husband to eat food out of restaurant trash bins and to sleep in a box on fisherman's wharf, then you've got to be someone very special."

Joan spoke next, "Shannon, I always wanted a sister, but I only got a brother, and he's always been in pain in my rear, trying to look out for me, so I know I can love you."

Michael was last to speak and said, "My dear Shannon, if you could put up with my father for all these months and still consider living with us, you must be an angel, and if I could have someone to help protect me from my dear little sister, you're really welcomed home."

Shannon could only stand there and cry; she had never before had a family with this kind of love. Michael was the first to reach for Shannon and held her in his arms and put her head on his shoulder, and that made her cry even harder.

Patricia came up to them and said, "Shannon, let me take you upstairs and find you a room."

Joan joined in and said, "I'll go with you and help find the perfect room just for you."

The three women went upstairs, and Patricia took Shannon to a room between Joan's and Michael's room. Patricia opened the door, and the three women walked into the largest bedroom Shannon had ever seen.

It was done in shades of green, and Patricia said, "I think because you're from Ireland, this room will be perfect for you."

Joan agreed, as did Shannon.

The bedroom had a closet larger than the two rooms John and she had been living in, and it had a bathroom like nothing she had ever seen in her life, with a huge bathtub and separate shower stall. Mirrors and lights were everywhere in the bathroom.

Patricia said, "If this room is OK, it's yours. If you don't like it, we have several more for you to choose from."

Shannon replied, "I love this room, and I don't know how to say how much I appreciate your kindness."

Patricia said, "I don't know how to thank you for everything you did for John. Words would never be enough to thank you for all the things I feel in my heart for you looking after John."

"I have to tell you, it soon became a mutual thing because before long, John was looking after me and helping me to get a real job. I think in the end, he saved me more than I saved him."

Joan said, "Thank you for all the things you did for Father. Tomorrow, we'll have to find you a dress so you can be one of my bridesmaids in my wedding next week."

"I can't do that. Tomorrow I have to work."

Patricia said, "OK, but you need to give them notice you're going to have to quit because you will have lots of things to do with us, you just won't have time to work. We have too many social and charitable jobs we have to do for the family."

"You expect me to do those things with you?"

"Of course, you will be part of our family, and we have so many obligations to help other people. John expects us to give at least 10 percent of our income to the church and another 10 percent to other charities, and with our family's income, it's a big job to do that every year. Plus, we'll have to get you a complete new wardrobe to carry out all this work. People expect us to look like we never wear the same dress twice, but of course, we do. Young lady, you don't know what kind of a family you've gotten yourself into."

Shannon said, "Yes, I do, it's a wonderful family!"

Shannon started crying again, and Patricia said, "Quit your crying, and let's go down for dinner."

15

SHANNON'S NEW WORLD

The next morning, Shannon woke up in her new bedroom and wondered where she was and where Michael was. Then she remembered Michael wasn't Michael Gilley. He was John Sterling, and this was his home, and he had a wife, Patricia; a son, Michael; and a daughter, Joan; and this was her new bedroom in John's home.

Shannon got up and went into her new bathroom and got into that huge bathtub and soaked for long time. When she was out of the bathtub and dried off, she found Joan had brought her one of her dresses to wear for the day. Now she remembered Joan giving it to her last night before she went to bed since she didn't yet have the few things from Michael's and her apartment.

She dressed and went downstairs to the dining room where they had dinner the night before; and the butler, Claude, saw her and said, "Ms. Shannon, the family is in the breakfast room."

Then he led her into the breakfast room, and there she was greeted by John, who got up from the table and gave Shannon a good morning hug and kissed her on her left cheek.

Shannon could only say, "Good morning, John."

Then she took a good look at John Sterling. He was now clean-shaven and dressed in a beautiful suit with a white shirt and red tie; she thought he looked twenty years younger.

Shannon said, "Wow, John, you look wonderful."

Patricia said, "Good morning, Shannon. How did you sleep, dear?" "Very well, and I loved my bath. I almost couldn't make myself get out of the tub. It felt so wonderful."

Joan joined in the conversation by saying, "Good morning, Shannon. I hope you feel like you are at home with us now."

"Oh, Joan, you all have treated me so well. I couldn't help but feel at home."

Then the last member of the family, Michael, came into the breakfast room and said, "Good morning, Shannon. Good morning, Father. It's so good to see you home, and good morning to you, Mom, and I guess to you, too, my little sister."

Joan laughed and replied, "Good of you to notice me too, big brother, now that I'm about to be an old married woman."

Michael joked, "Oh, I forgot to tell you, Robert called and said the wedding is off. He doesn't have time right now. He's too busy at the office."

Joan responded, "He'll be too busy looking after me to be working at that office in a few days."

John asked, "So when is this wedding taking place?"

Joan answered, "Well, if you can keep from getting lost, it will be Saturday. So I want you to stay at home, so Mother can watch you all the time until after my wedding."

John said, "I will do my very best not to get lost before your wedding."

Patricia replied, "You better not be getting lost, ever again." "No, dear, I won't ever get lost again."

Everyone agreed that would be a very good idea.

After everyone finished their breakfast, Shannon said, "I do have to go to work today and talk to my boss and let him know I will be quitting as soon as they can find someone to take my place."

Patricia said, "OK, Shannon, but I hope they can find someone very soon because I'm going to need your help with Joan getting married and going off on her honeymoon."

"OK, Patricia, I'll try to let them know they need to get someone very soon because I need to help you."

Patricia asked, "Shannon, could you call me Mom or Mother? I would like that very much."

Shannon began to tear up, and Patricia said, "Now don't you start crying again. You're home and you will be just fine, my dear Shannon."

Shannon replied, "Yes, Mother."

John said, "That's sounds better, and you can call me Dad or Father instead of John. Because I know you would be trying to call me Michael, and now that I know my name, I probably wouldn't answer to Michael."

Michael piped in and said, "You can call me Michael or Mike as some of my friends do. Just don't call me late for dinner."

They all laughed at what Michael said.

Then Michael said, "Shannon, I'm on my way to work. I'll drop you off at the Harbor Police Department. I know your boss, Chief Stone. His wife is a very good friend of Joan's. How Joan has any friends, no one will ever know."

Joan said, "Go to work, Michael, and don't let the door hit you in the butt as you go out the door."

Then Michael went over to Joan and gave her a kiss right on her mouth and said, "I'm going to miss you when you're gone." Then he hugged Joan's neck and said, "Shannon, if you are ready, let's get out of here before my sister thinks of some great comeback."

Michael took Shannon's hand and said, "Come with me to the carriage, my dear sister, and we'll fly away to work."

Hand in hand, Michael and Shannon went out the front door and boarded the horse-drawn carriage waiting for them at the curb. Michael said to the driver as he helped Shannon into the carriage, "Charles, we need to go by the docks to take Ms. Shannon to her job at the Harbor Police Department."

Then Michael got into the carriage and sat next to Shannon.

Michael said, "Shannon, I wanted to tell you how much I appreciate you looking after my father when he was hurt and when he didn't have any idea who he was. My father is like me. He has always had servants to look after us. I can't imagine my father eating food from trash bins and living in a box on the fishermen's docks. After you ladies went up to your bedrooms, Father told me all about you finding him and taking care of his wound and looking after him. He thinks you are wonderful and loves you very much."

"That's very nice of you to say that, but your father helped me to get a job and how to feel like I was worth something and not just a jilted Irish girl with no home and no future. It did a lot for me, and I love him like the father I never had."

"How about your mother? Did she raise you by herself?"

"No, I was raised by nuns. I was an orphan, as my mother died when I was born, at least that was what I was told. Maybe she just didn't want me. I don't know, and I have no idea who my father was either."

"You've haven't had a lot of luck in your life, have you, Shannon?"

"No, I guess I haven't, but I was certainly lucky to find your father and help him. He's done more for me than anyone else in my life. I had no idea he had anything but what little clothes he had on when I found him lying in that alley. I certainly never expected him to have a fine home and a wonderful family. Your mother is so nice, and your sister has treated me like I was part of the family. I can't believe the way you all have treated me."

Michael said, "We love our father. He's such a wonderful man, and he does so much for so many people. I guess you were sent by God to help him when he really needed help for the first time in his life. Father believes that there are no accidental things that happen and that God has a plan for each of us in our life, and when Father was robbed and hurt, it was no accident. It was God's plan for you to meet him. Father thinks you were sent for some special reason to our family."

"So what do you think? Do you think I was sent for some special reason to your family?"

"Maybe you are. I just don't know what it is yet."

When they arrived at the Harbor Police Department, Michael got out of the carriage and helped Shannon out and asked what time she got off work and told her he would be back with the carriage if he could get his work finished. He said if he was still working, he would send the carriage back to take her home; either way, he would see her tonight.

Shannon told Chief Stone about what had happened to her after she went home last night. He was very pleased for her and told her the Sterlings were one of the finest families in New York. He said he would be seeing her at Joan's wedding and that Michael Sterling was a very fine young man.

Rocky said, "I know just the person to take your job, Mrs. O'Rourke.

She certainly needs a job since her husband, Officer O'Rourke, was killed, and you're going to be kept very busy helping Mrs. Sterling with all her work. Shannon, I want you to know how much we appreciate you getting everything for the employees' records organized so well when you started working here. You did a great job. Thank you."

Rocky sent one of his officers to ask Mrs. O'Rourke to meet with him as soon as she could since he had a job for her. One hour later, the officer returned with Mrs. O'Rourke to see Chief Stone, and he offered her Shannon's job. She was concerned she might not be good enough to do the work since she had never worked outside the home. Rocky assured her that since Shannon had set up everything so well, she shouldn't have any problem doing the job and that Shannon would be able to teach her what she needed to know. Rocky introduced Mrs. O'Rourke to Shannon and asked Shannon to work with her and show her how to do the job.

Shannon asked Mrs. O'Rourke what her first name was, and she said her name was Mary. Shannon suggested that she would make it easier to tell everyone her name was Mary because she would fit in better with the rest of the people she would be working with. Mary liked that idea, and from then on, she would introduce herself as Mary O'Rourke.

Shannon spent the rest of the day explaining each of the forms she made and how to fill out each form and what she had to do with each one.

By the end of the day, Shannon had written down information on each of the forms and what the distribution was of each one of the forms. Shannon told her the most important form was the payroll form because if that form wasn't done, no one would get paid, and she wouldn't be very popular with the rest of the employees. Mary assured her she would make sure she had that form filled out and turned in on time because she certainly didn't want to be responsible for causing people not to get paid.

A little after three, Shannon left her job at the Harbor Police Department for the last time. It seemed like everything worked out very well for everyone. She had a new family to live with, and Mary had a new job. Maybe John Sterling was right, God had a plan for everyone.

When Shannon went out of the Harbor Police Station, a coach and Michael Sterling were waiting for her to take her to her new life.

16

GETTING READY FOR JOAN'S WEDDING

The Sterling household was a beehive of activity with everybody busy getting ready for Joan's postponed wedding.

The staff was cleaning everything inside and outside the house as if it wasn't always sparkling clean. Patricia decided to hold the wedding reception at their home instead of at the restaurant where they had originally planned to have it. Many of the guests wouldn't have had an opportunity to visit their home before, and since she decided to hold the guest list for the wedding and reception to only one hundred guests, she felt it wouldn't be a problem having the reception in their back garden. They would have their guests seated in a large tent in their backyard, adjacent to their kitchen, so it would be easy for the staff to serve directly from the kitchen.

Their house was designed for easy access from the kitchen, dining room, and library to the terrace outside in the back garden because Mr. Sterling enjoyed having breakfast there and going out to look at their lovely grounds. Patricia arranged for a company to set up the tent the Monday before the wedding was to be held on the following Saturday. The same company would also be providing the tables and the chairs for the reception.

Early Monday morning, the crew arrived to begin setting up the tent.

Patricia had no idea of the amount of work required to set up the large tent. She knew she needed a large tent but had no idea of how much space in her back garden the tent would require. Not only did it cover the area directly behind the kitchen, it also covered the areas coming from the dining room and the library; in fact, it was almost as wide as the entire back of their house. It took the crew almost six hours to erect the tent and have it securely fastened down.

When they were finished, Patricia looked out of her bedroom window and thought it looked like someone had left a really big white fluffy pillow covering most of her back garden. Patricia met with the foreman of the job and checked the tent over with its system of supports inside the tent and found the tent had only four large poles in the very center of the tent required to hold up the big tent. She found they had laid a wooden floor over the grass and then covered the floor with a very plush carpet and had it securely fastened, so no one would be tripping over it.

Patricia was very pleased with the way the tent looked and told the foreman he and his men did a fine job and she was very happy with their work. The foreman told her they would bring the tables and chairs the next day and would get them all set up, and then they could spend time discussing how she thought the chairs and tables should be arranged. The discussion lasted for some time, but Patricia finally decided to try the way the foreman suggested, and then she would look at the layout and make a decision if she felt the arrangement needed any changes.

The chef told Patricia he would need some extra help preparing the meal, and the butler said he needed additional help serving the meal.

Patricia suggested to the butler, Claude, he should make the arrangements for whatever help he and Chef Charles needed. After Patricia thought about it for a minute, she suggested Claude call his friend, the director of dining at the Waldorf Astoria Hotel, and see if he could get some of his staff who might like to earn some extra money to help them. She said if he had some people available, they would have experience serving, which would be a big help, and maybe he had some people from their kitchen that could also help the chef.

Patricia and Joan had spent a long time planning the menu for the reception dinner. Claude told Patricia he thought she had a good idea and would contact his friend at the Waldorf to see if he could help them out.

The flowers were to be brought early Saturday morning, and Claude would take care of their placement in the tent and in the various downstairs rooms.

The wedding cake had been ordered again, and it was to be a sevenlayered white heart-shaped cake with white icing, the same kind of cake they ordered the first time. Joan was hoping this time they had a chance to actually eat a piece of the cake.

The church was booked, and their minister was set to do their wedding. They had a very good band and two singers booked for the reception. As far as Patricia and Joan were concerned, they had everything planned for the wedding and the reception. The only thing they knew they had left to do was to have a bridesmaid dress made for Shannon to match the other bridesmaids' dresses.

Joan's bridesmaids were Serene as maid of honor, Latesha, and Shannon. Robert's groomsmen were Indian as best man, Michael, and Rocky. Joan wondered that now that her father was home, what else could possibly go wrong to postpone her wedding. Robert had been so patient, and his folks had been here such a very long time. Joan knew Serene and Indian needed to get back to their ranch in Texas. Joan was certain nothing could stop the wedding this time, she hoped.

They still needed to get Shannon's dress finished for the wedding, and they needed to buy her a new wardrobe. Joan thought it would be fun helping a sister buy all the new clothes that she would need to be dressed as Father would want her to be.

Life was a funny thing. Joan always wanted to have a little sister to be with, and it only took her father to be robbed, hit in the head, not know who he was for months, to bring home a young woman who had helped take care of him through all that. Now, Shannon was going to be her sister and living in a home and having a family. Shannon had never had a home or a family of her own before, and it was very hard for someone like Joan to understand that, but now Joan had the sister she always wanted. Shannon was only a couple of years younger than she was, but Joan knew Shannon had a lot to learn as far as being in the eyes of New York's society and in the New York newspapers.

Joan had grown up being in the spotlight since she was the daughter of one of the wealthiest families in the country and her grandfather, her mother's father, was Bob Wagoner, a United States senator. Shannon was definitely going to need Joan's help to adjust to her new life.

Joan knew the first thing Shannon needed to know for her new life was where to go shopping, so she told Shannon, "We need to begin your education today about where you need to go shopping." Joan and Shannon spent the day going from store to store, buying a complete new wardrobe for Shannon and introducing Shannon to the owners or the managers of the stores. When they finished shopping in each store Joan would ask the store to please deliver their purchases to their home.

Shannon had never had such a day in her life. She told Joan shopping was harder than working; the only break she got for the day was an hour for lunch. By the time they returned home, Shannon was completely exhausted, and she sat down on the first couch she could find in the library. Joan could have been ready to go shopping for several more hours. She was a truly a veteran shopper.

Not long after the shoppers returned home, John and Michael arrived home from their office and went straight into the library to speak to Shannon.

Michael said, "Shannon, Father and I have some things we need to tell you. I will go first." Michael took a package out of his briefcase and walked over to Shannon and handed her the package and said, "Shannon, because you were the person responsible for finding and bringing Father home, you will find in this package, a checkbook and a savings account book. We have deposited $10,000 in your checking account and $90,000 in your savings account, the reward offered for returning Father safely home."

Shannon replied, "Michael, I don't deserve the reward. Your father found his own way home. I just came along with him."

John replied, "Shannon, not only do you deserve the reward, but you earned it, and one more thing I want to say. I had my attorney draw up adoption papers for Mother and me to sign to legally adopt you if you are willing to let us. Shannon, are you willing to let us to adopt you?"

Shannon began to cry.

John took her into his arms to comfort her.

Through her tears, Shannon replied, "Yes, oh, yes, it would be wonderful if you adopted me."

Michael replied, "Well, I'm sorry for you. You have no idea how bad this family really is that you're to become a part of."

Joan added, "That's right, Shannon. We're a bad bunch, and you're about to have a half-blooded Indian for a brother-in-law. That's right! You haven't met Robert yet. Maybe I'm not going to introduce you to him until after we're married. He might decide he wants my younger sister instead of me."

Shannon laughed, and Patricia said, "Shannon, this family is not as bad as these people say. Actually, the younger ones are much worse than your new parents. I really have no idea of how these two turned out so bad. It must have been all those teachers they had because I know for a fact their parents are perfect."

John said, "Well, now we have a chance to improve our record with our new daughter. Shannon, all you need to do is to sign the adoption papers, and our lawyer can get them filed with the court tomorrow and you will soon legally be a Sterling."

Shannon replied, "I don't know why I have been so blessed since I came to America, but I will be so happy to be a Sterling, thank you. Thank you, all."

17

WHATEVER CAN GO WRONG, WILL

Thursday morning, Robert telephoned Indian at his suite at the Waldorf Astoria and asked Indian if he could meet him because he had something to tell him. Indian told Robert he'd be happy to meet with him for lunch. They made an appointment to meet at the dining room at Indian's hotel at twelve-thirty.

After Indian hung up the phone from talking with Robert, he said, "Serene, I just talked to Robert, and he said he wanted to talk with me today about something, but he didn't say what he wanted to talk about."

"Indian, maybe he needed to talk to you about his wedding night."

"Well, I don't know how I would talk to him about that. I'm sure not an expert on those kinds of things."

Serene replied, "Well, you have had a wedding night and he hasn't. I think you know a lot about making love. Anyway, I like the way you do it."

"Well, doing it is one thing. Talking about it to some other man is just not my thing."

"Cheer up, love. Don't get all upset about something you don't have any idea about what he wants to talk to you about. Maybe he just wants to tell you about what he's planning for their honeymoon and wants you to tell him if it sounds OK. Indian, I know you don't like things you haven't planned out, but sometimes you just need to go with the flow."

"OK, Serene, but it's going to be a long morning, trying to figure out what he wants to talk to me about."

"Yes, dear, for you it will be, but remember, he's your best friend." By eleven-thirty, Indian said, "Serene, I'm going on down to the dining room to wait for Robert. I don't want him to have to wait for me."

"OK, Indian, if it will make you feel better, go on down and wait in the dining room for Robert. Indian, I'll see you later. Latesha is on her way to pick me up. We have to go to Joan's house to try on our bridesmaid's dresses to make sure they fit OK. I love you, so please quit fretting about what Robert wants to talk to you about. He'll be here in a few minutes."

"Yes, dear, go try on your new dress and tell Joan and Latesha hello for me."

Indian went out the door and onto the elevator and quickly made his way to the dining room and found Robert standing there waiting for him.

Robert said, "Indian, I'm really glad to see you. I need to talk with you about a big problem."

Indian said, "OK, Robert. I'm glad to see you too, so what's your big problem? Is it something about your wedding?"

"Yes, it is. I think we should go somewhere more private to discuss this problem."

Indian thought, Oh no, he wants to talk about the wedding night. Oh, God, why me?

"OK, Robert, we can go up to our suite, and you can tell me all about your big problem. I'll see if I can help you. Serene was just leaving to go with Latesha over to go your bride's house to try on their bridesmaid's dresses."

Indian and Robert took an elevator up to the floor of Indian's suite.

They left the elevator and walked to Indian and Serene's suite. Indian unlocked the door, and he and Robert went inside. Once inside the suite, Indian asked Robert to sit down and tell him what the big problem was.

Robert said, "Indian, I got a call this morning from a woman who said she knew a man who was planning on kill Joan during our wedding."

"Who was this woman, Robert?"

"I have no idea. She just said a man she knows very well was planning on killing Joan during her wedding."

"She didn't say why he wanted to kill her?"

"No, she just said she called to warn me not to go through with the wedding because this man had promised he would kill her."

"Who else have you talked to about this?"

"Nobody, just you, Indian. I didn't know what we should do." "I would say the first thing we need to do is to get everybody together and talk about your call. Robert, call John Sterling and ask him to get the family together for an emergency meeting about your wedding. After you talk to him, ask how long it will be before he can get all the family there.

I'll call Rocky Stone and ask him to come to the Sterling home and be there for the meeting."

Robert telephoned John Sterling and told him that there was a major problem with the wedding that's scheduled for Saturday, and he needed him to get all the family together to discuss the problem. After the call, John seemed worried, but he wasn't sure what he was worried about. He did what Robert asked him to do, and he set up the time for the meeting at two o'clock. John called Robert back at Indian's suite and told him the meeting was set for two o'clock.

After Indian knew what time John set the meeting for, to discuss this new problem, Indian called Rocky at the Harbor Police Headquarters and asked him to come to the Sterling home for a two o'clock meeting about a new problem with Robert and Joan's wedding.

Two o'clock came and everyone was there, including Robert's parents, waiting for Indian and Robert to tell them what this new problem was all about.

Indian begin the meeting saying, "I'm sorry to have to ask everyone to drop what they were doing and come for a meeting about some new problem with Robert and Joan's wedding, but this is potentially a lifethreatening problem. I'm going to ask Robert to tell you what happened this morning at work that has prompted this meeting. Robert, please tell everyone what happened."

Robert got up and said, "A few minutes after I got to my office this morning, I received a telephone call from a very upset woman who told me I had to cancel my wedding because a man she knows very well has promised to kill Joan during the wedding. She wouldn't tell me who she was. She just repeated it before hanging up the telephone, he is going to kill Joan."

Indian got back up and said, "Frankly, I would say that people like Rocky and I know if someone threatens to kill someone and they're willing to give up their life to do it, it's almost impossible to stop them. That's why I asked Robert to get everybody together so you can decide what you want to do about the wedding."

Joan popped up and said, "Oh no, we're not canceling my wedding again.

Indian said, "Joan, what if we couldn't stop them from killing you?"

"Well, at least I'd die a married woman." Robert said, "Joan, you don't mean that."

"I certainly do."

Indian asked, "So what are the options for you two to get married?"

Patricia said, "Well, I would say we could move the wedding to our house and only have the family attend."

Joan said, "Mother, you know I've always planned to be married in our church."

"Yes, I know, dear, but I'd much rather have you married and alive."

Joan asked, "Indian, Rocky, what could you do to help me have the wedding I've always dreamed about in my church?"

Rocky said, "Well, we could set up security at the church and during your travel back and forth from your house to the church and then back here for your reception. However, this still wouldn't guarantee your safety completely, but it would make it much harder for someone to kill you. Do you agree, Indian?"

"Well, it would make it less likely, but again, if someone is willing to give up their life, there's no guarantee that he still might be able to kill you."

Joan said, "Well, you two will have to do the best you can to keep me alive through my wedding."

Indian said, "Rocky, I guess if Joan is determined to go ahead with her wedding in the church, I guess we will have to try to set up security the best we can to keep her from being killed."

"OK, Indian, we might as well end this meeting, and the two of us will go off on our own to figure out the best plan we can to keep her safe."

Indian said, "You're right."

Rocky and Indian left to devise the best plan they could to keep Joan safe. When they left, the meeting broke up and the rest of the people went back to what they had been involved in before Robert's call.

Shannon's bridesmaid dress had been completed but not delivered. Serene and Latesha tried on their dresses, but neither of them fit right; the dresses were far too large.

Patricia telephoned the lady who was in charge of making Shannon's dress, and she said she just found out her helpers mixed up the measurements with another order for bridesmaids' dresses that were not due until next week. The lady said she would bring two of her dressmakers over to the house right away and have them fix the dresses and bring Shannon's dress.

So what else could go wrong?

Sometimes you don't even want to know!

Chef Charles came into the library looking for Patricia as Joan, Serene, Latesha, and Shannon were waiting for the dressmakers to come to fix their dresses. Joan could tell looking at Charles's face something was wrong and asked, "What's wrong, Charles?"

"What's wrong? What's wrong is that the people from the market delivered my order and only half of the things I need for your reception is here. I don't know what I'm going to do."

"Charles, I'll find Mother and have her come to the kitchen. I'm sure she can help you."

"I hope so. I can't fix the things we planned for your reception if I don't have the all the ingredients to make them, can I?"

"No, Charles, I'm sure you can't, but I'll find Mother. I'm sure between you and her, everything will be all right. You go back to the kitchen and do what you can and I'll find Mother."

Charles turned around and made his way to the kitchen, and Joan left to find her mother. Joan soon found her mother and explained the problem Chef Charles was having.

Patricia said, "I'll go to see Charles after I call our market."

Patricia telephoned the market whom they had been working with for years and asked to speak to the manager. Soon the market manager, Jack Robinson, answered the telephone and asked who he was speaking with.

Patricia said, "Mr. Robinson, this is Patricia Sterling calling, and my chef, Charles, just informed me that half of the order he placed with you that he needs for my daughter's wedding reception is missing."

"Oh, Mrs. Sterling, may I please call you back in a few minutes? I'll need to check with the folks who have been preparing your order to see what the problem is."

"Certainly, Mr. Robinson, we have always enjoyed your service. I'm sure you can take care of whatever the problem is."

"Yes, Mrs. Sterling, we have appreciated your business for a long time. I will call you back in a few minutes."

Patricia hung up the telephone, and less than five minutes later, butler Claude said, "Mrs. Sterling, Mr. Robinson with the market is on the telephone for you."

"Thank you, Claude."

Patricia picked up the telephone and said, "Mr. Robinson, what have you found out about the other half of our order that's missing?"

"I'm sorry to say, but we have a new delivery man who just didn't see all your orders. He is loading it in the delivery carriage now and should be at your house in a very few minutes. I'm very sorry for it being delayed, Mrs. Sterling. I think this thunderstorm has everyone a little off right now. Anyway, you should have the rest of your order in just a few minutes."

"Thank you for your help in this matter, Mr. Robinson." "Thank you, Mrs. Sterling. We have appreciated your business for many years now."

Patricia hung up the telephone as Claude was answering the front door, and the dressmakers were there with Shannon's dress and they were ready to alter the bridesmaids' dresses for Serene and Latesha. Patricia heard a loud clap of thunder and looked out in the back garden and saw lightning strike the big tent, and she saw that it was on fire. Patricia went out into the back garden and found a garden hose that was being used to water some plants and directed the water onto the fire on the tent, but the fire was spreading faster than she could put it out.

Patricia yelled at Claude to call the fire department. She continued trying to contain the fire with her garden hose until she heard the fire wagon out in the front of the house. By now, Joan had joined her in the back garden.

Patricia said, "Joan, open up the garden gates and show the firemen where the fire is."

Joan opened the gates, and the firemen rushed in with their much bigger hoses, but Patricia stayed right with the firemen as she pointed out places where the fire had spread. Finally, the fire was out but the tent was a total wreck.

The fire chief recognized Patricia Sterling from seeing her pictures in the society pages and thanked her for helping them.

He took off his fire chief helmet and placed it on her head and said, "As the fire chief of the City of New York, I hereby make you the first woman to officially become a fireman for the City of New York." By this time, not only were the firemen in Patricia's back garden, but several newspaper reporters were, and they took pictures of Patricia with black smoke stains all over her face and hair, wearing her fire chief's helmet, which would be on the front pages of several of New York's newspapers the next morning.

Patricia thanked the firemen for putting out the fire and said, "If there is anything I can do for you, just let me know."

As she was trying to give back the fire chief's helmet, which he wouldn't take, one fireman yelled out, "You can talk to the mayor about getting us a raise."

Patricia replied, "I'll see what I can do about that."

The firemen picked up their hoses and began getting all their equipment out of her back garden.

Patricia went back into the house and called the tent rental company and said, "Lighting hit our tent and caught it on fire, and I'm sorry to say it's been completely destroyed. We need another tent put up tonight for the wedding reception tomorrow."

Less than two hours later, whatever was left of the old tent had been hauled away and a new one was being put up. By ten o'clock that night, the new tent was up, and everything that had been lost on the inside of the old tent had been replaced.

Joan said, "Mother, you're unbelievable. I'll never be able to take care of everything like you do."

"Don't worry, dear. You just need to learn you can do whatever it takes to get the job done."

18

SECURITY FOR THE WEDDING

Indian and Rocky went to Rocky's father-in-law's home, where he and Latesha were living while she was working to help her father with all his investments being used to develop new inventions.

They made their way into Rocky's office and began to formulate a security plan to keep Joan safe at her wedding.

Indian said, "Rocky, we are going to need several men to help provide enough security to keep Joan alive, not only at the church, but going and coming from the church. In addition to that, we need to have security at the reception in the Sterling home."

"Indian, I'll ask some of the men from the Harbor police if they would like to earn some extra money helping us."

"That's a good idea. I think we might be able to get by with, say, six or seven men along with us, don't you think, Rocky?"

"Yes, I'm sure we can if we move them around. We could have some of the men prepositioned at the church and the others guarding Joan on the way to the church and back to the house. Then, when we're traveling back to the house, the men inside the church could get back to the house before the bride and groom arrive and set up security at the house."

"Rocky, I think that should work. One thing I'm going to suggest is that the groom and his groomsmen wear Western wear and carry our six-guns. I didn't want to wear that silly-looking suit they had for me anyway, and now we have a perfect excuse to wear our regular clothes, so we can have our guns handy."

"Great idea! I know you and I have our Western wear, but how about Robert and Michael?"

"I know Robert has his, so that's no problem. For Michael, though, I doubt if he has ever had on anything like what we wear." Rocky said, "Michael is about my height and weight. I've got plenty of Western dress clothes he could wear. Don't know about the boots though, but maybe he can wear a pair of my boots all right."

"Rocky, I don't think the women are going to be happy about us wearing our Western wear. I'm pretty sure they were looking forward seeing us in those monkey suits."

"You're probably right, Indian. So you can tell them that we need to wear our six-shooters, so we can get to them in a hurry."

"Thanks, Rocky, you're all heart."

"Think nothing of it, Indian, glad to help out anytime."

Then Rocky laughed and Indian kind of looked off into space.

Next, Rocky called the Harbor police office and said, "This is Chief Stone, and I need to talk to Captain Sean O'Malley."

A short time later, Sean answered the telephone and asked, "What can I do for you, Chief?"

"Sean, I need six men and you on Saturday to help with security for a wedding at the Sterling home. I'm here with Indian Leader, and we're working on setting up security for his friend, Robert Smiley's, wedding to Ms. Joan Sterling. You can tell the men they will be paid double their daily wages working this wedding. I think you know the address of the Sterlings since that's where Shannon lives now."

"What time do you wants us there on Saturday, Chief?" "Seven a.m. Indian and I will be waiting for you at the front of the house."

"Right, and yes, I do have the Sterlings' address. Shannon left her address and telephone number in case Mary O'Rourke had any problems filling out any of the forms. She said she left the information in case she needed to get in touch with her."

"OK, Sean, we'll see you Saturday morning."

Indian and Rocky went back to the Sterlings to talk to their wives and to tell Robert that they thought it best for Joan's security for them to wear their Western dress clothes, along with their guns, on Saturday and have him and Michael wear Western clothes too. Before they went back to the Sterlings, Rocky picked out one set of his best Western dress clothes for Michael, along with a pair of new cowboy boots that he had never worn.

When they returned to the Sterlings, they arrived at the same time as Patricia's father, Senator Wagner, and his aide, Larry Larson.

Patricia introduced Rocky and Indian to the senator and his aide.

Patricia said, "Father, someone has threatened to kill Joan at her wedding, and Rocky and Indian are organizing security for Joan." "Patricia, why didn't you tell me this before? I would have telephoned the mayor of New York City and had their police provide security for my granddaughter."

"Father, my family has been in the newspapers enough with John being missing, and then earlier this evening, lightning struck the reception tent in our back garden and burned it to the ground. When the fire department finished putting out the fire, because I stayed out there helping the firemen, the fire chief made me the first woman fireman in New York City and gave me his helmet. There were several reporters taking my picture with my fire chief's helmet on. I'm sure it will be in the newspapers in the morning. See, Father, sitting on the table over there, is my fire helmet."

"OK, Patricia, I promise I won't call the mayor and ask him to send a bunch of police officers to protect my granddaughter."

"Father, you haven't met your new granddaughter yet, have you?" "Lord, what is going on with your family? I'm getting a grandson who's half Indian, and now you tell me I have a new granddaughter.

Did Michael get married and no one told me?"

"No, Father, Michael hasn't gotten married. Your new granddaughter is the young woman who took care of John when he had no idea of who he was. You'll love her just like we all do."

Shannon came into the library where all of them were gathered, and Patricia said, "There she is, Father. Shannon, please come over and meet my father, Bob Wagner, your grandfather."

Shannon walked over and said, "How do you do, Mr. Wagner?" Senator Wagner looked at Shannon and replied, "Well, young lady.

I never expected to meet a new granddaughter who was a full-grown woman, no, never. Normally, a new granddaughter comes about a few inches long and around six or seven pounds.

But I must say. I see I have a very beautiful young lady for my new granddaughter. Welcome to the family, my dear."

Senator Wagner reached out his arms and gave Shannon a very big hug.

Indian watched Senator Wagner's aide, Larry Larson, who seemed to be very upset about everything that was going on; and when drinks were offered to everyone, Larry took his drink and went off away from the family and sat down on a couch on the other side of the room. Indian kept watching him, wondering what his problem was, and saw him get another drink.

After Indian saw that Larry had almost finished his second drink, he went over and sat down with him and asked, "What do you think about this wedding of Senator Wagner's granddaughter?" "Well, I've told the senator he needs to stop this marriage because when he runs for president, there are too many people's votes he is going to lose because too many people's loved ones in this country have been killed by Indians. Tonight, I see his daughter has an Irish woman as an adopted daughter. Too many people in New York hate those people coming in taking their jobs because they are willing to work for less money. He might as well forget running for president now. I can't believe he can't control his own family. After all the years I've given him, to just throw it all away. What we've worked for up to now is a total waste."

Larry went over, got another drink, and drank it straight down. Then he walked over to where the senator was sitting and said, "You're just going to sit there and let your granddaughter marry a damned redskin? Then she'll spit out a bunch of half-breed kids, and it just throws away your chance of becoming the president of the United States, and for what? Does she think that redskin is the only man she could marry to make her happy? He's not. Almost anybody would be better for her and for us."

Senator Wagner said, "Larry, you've been with me a long time, so you need to apologize to my granddaughter and her mother or your time with me is over."

"I wouldn't apologize to these people. They're not fit to shine my shoes. They can all go to hell as far as I'm concerned because that's where they all belong."

Rocky was standing close by and reached over and took Larry by the arm and pulled him over to the library door, and then took him out the front door and asked his coachman if he would take this man to his home.

The coachman said, "Yes, sir."

Rocky pushed Larry inside the coach and said, "Tell the coachman where you live."

Rocky heard Larry give the coachman an address, and away they went. Rocky went back inside the house and joined the others in the library.

He heard Senator Wagner say, "I've known Larry since he graduated from Harvard. I've never known him to say a bad word about anybody, much less about my family."

Indian said, "Senator, your man was drinking a lot in just a few minutes. I'd guess he wasn't used to drinking, and it was the drink that caused such an outburst."

"Well, that may be true, but sometimes drinking lets you say things that you really believe when, otherwise, you never would. I'm afraid he said what he really thinks about my family."

Patricia said, "Dad, I think you should stay here tonight, so you're not going home to that great big house all by yourself. You can stay in the big bedroom we have on this floor, so you don't have to climb stairs. In fact, why don't you get rid of that big old house and move in with us all the time? Besides, you spend more time in Washington than you do here, so it makes sense if you just get rid of your house."

"Patricia, you're right. Where's Joan? I want to tell her something."

"She and Robert went to check about something. They should be right back. In fact, she and Robert are coming back in here right now."

Patricia said, "Joan, come here. Your grandfather has something to tell you."

Joan and Robert walked over to where her mother and grandfather were standing.

Senator Wagner said, "Sit down, you two. I have something I want to tell you. I have decided to move in with your parents, and I want to give you and Robert a wedding present."

"Thank you, Grandfather."

"Joan, I'm giving you my house as your wedding present. The only thing you can't have is my butler, Watson. You'll have to get your own butler. Watson will be coming here with me as my valet, if that's all right with your mother."

Patricia said, "Of course, it's all right with me."

Senator Wagner said, "Then it's all settled. The house is yours, Joan."

Before the party was over, Rocky said to Indian, "You haven't told the women about the change in our wardrobe yet."

Serene, Latesha, and Joan were all standing just a little away from Indian and Rocky and heard what Rocky had to say.

Serene asked, "So, Indian, what were you going to tell us about the change in your wardrobe for the wedding?"

Indian looked at Rocky, and Rocky said, "Go ahead, Indian, tell them."

Indian blurted out, "We're going to be wearing our Western dress clothes, so we can wear our six-shooters to help with the security for Joan. Rocky and I agreed it would be too hard wearing those monkey suits to have our guns handy in case we needed them to protect Joan."

Robert said, "I agree, we need to be able to get to our guns, and wearing those tuxes would make it too difficult."

Joan asked, "What's Michael going to wear?"

Rocky replied, "I brought some new Western clothes for him and a pair of new boots."

Michael came up to join in this conversation and asked, "You want me to dress in Western clothes for Joan's wedding?"

Robert answered, "Yes, we do, so you'll match the kind of clothes the rest of us in the wedding will be wearing. Rocky brought you a complete Western outfit, including cowboy boots."

"OK, I can do that. I hope they'll fit me."

Rocky said, "I think you are about the same size as I am, so they should fit you. I gave the clothes and boots to Claude when we arrived and asked him to have them taken up to your room."

Michael replied, "OK, I can try them on in the morning, and if they have to be altered a little, I'm sure one of the maids can do it."

Indian said, "OK, I guess that's all settled then."

Serene said, "Wait a minute, it's not settled. What does Joan think about the change in your wardrobe?"

Every eye in the room was on Joan, waiting to hear what she would say about changing her plans for the wedding.

Joan finally answered, "I had planned for Robert and his groomsmen to wear the tuxes, but I understand Indian's point.

Besides, I fell in love with Robert when Western clothes were the only clothes he owned, so it's really the right thing to do."

Indian said again, "Then it's all settled. We're wearing Western clothes so Rocky and I can quickly get to our six-shooters to help protect Joan."

19

THE WEDDING DAY

Friday, the day before Joan and Robert's wedding, Indian and Rocky spent time going to the church to see where they would post the security men both outside and inside the church and to check how long it would take the wedding party to travel to and from the church. They decided they would have Sean O'Malley stationed in the balcony at the front of the church where he would have a clear view of the all the church below him. They also planned to have the balcony closed off, so no one other than Sean could be upstairs. The time it took them from the Sterling home to the church was almost twenty minutes and almost twenty-five minutes coming back. They agreed it was going to be almost impossible to protect Joan going and coming from the house to the church and back. The best they thought they could do was to have some men riding alongside the carriage to keep someone from shooting at Joan. The other thing was the woman told Robert the man planned to kill Joan at the wedding, so maybe it wasn't as important to try to protect her going to and coming from the church. They also checked to see how Michael was making out with the Western clothes Rocky had brought him.

When they went to the Sterlings', they asked the butler, Claude, if he could ask Michael to come to see them. They wanted to see how he was doing with the clothing Rocky brought him.

Claude went up to Michael's room and returned and said, "Mr. Michael asked me to bring you up to his room to visit with him."

They followed Claude to Michael's room, and when they arrived, Claude knocked on his door and they heard Michael say, "Come in."

Claude opened the door, and Michael was in his closet. Claude said, "Mr. Michael, your guests are here."

"Thank you, Claude."

Claude left the room, and Michael came out of his closet wearing his Western dress clothes, including his cowboy boots.

Rocky said, "Good morning, cowboy. You look just fine."

Michael smiled and said, "Thank you, Rocky. The clothes fit fine. However, I have to learn to walk in these boots. I like them. In fact, if I can get used to them, I may only wear cowboy boots from now on. I think they make me taller."

Indian replied, "Yeah, they do make you look taller."

Rocky said, "I think you should just start wearing them all the time."

Michael replied, "Are you two making fun of me?"

Indian said, "Michael, why would we do that? Man, we've been wearing boots all our lives. We didn't know there was any other kind of footwear. Serene bought me a pair of fancy shoes that you had to tie up to keep them on your feet. They didn't last a day before I was back in my boots."

Michael replied, "I'm going to wear the boots all day to get used to walking in them so I don't fall down at Joan's wedding."

Rocky said, "You'll be fine. I just wanted to see if you thought the clothes looked all right before Indian and I finished our security plan for tomorrow."

Rocky and Indian left Michael's room and spent an hour going over everything they planned for Joan's security for her wedding.

Indian finally said, "I don't think we can do any more to assure that Joan makes it through her wedding tomorrow."

Rocky agreed, and they left the Sterlings' house to go to meet their wives.

Indian said, "I'll see you tomorrow morning at six-thirty right here."

"OK, cowboy. See you at 6:30 a.m."

The next morning, a few minutes before six-thirty, Rocky and Indian met in the front of the Sterlings' home. A few minutes later, Sean O'Malley and six Harbor police officers arrived at the Sterlings' front door. Rocky and Indian greeted their friends and all the officers said their good morning.

Indian said, "Captain O'Malley, I want you to take three of your officers to come with me to the church, and I'll show you where I want to position each of you at the church. Rocky will work with you other three men here inside the house to protect Joan Sterling before she leaves for the church and when the wedding party returns from the church. OK, Sean, pick out your three men, and we'll take a couple of carriages and go to the church."

They had made arrangements yesterday to have someone at the church by 7:00 a.m. to let them inside, so Indian could position his men inside the church. The five of them loaded into the carriages, and the coachmen drove them to the church. Indian had asked Sean to ride in his carriage so they could talk about the problem with protecting Joan on the way to and from the church. They both agreed it was going to be hard to do with so many buildings along the route, with two or more stories in height.

Sean said, "Once, when I was with the Dublin Police Department, I had the responsibility of protecting the prime minister of England who was on a visit there. As you may know, the prime minister of England was not a favorite person in Ireland, so it was a big job to provide him with security.

To protect him in his carriage, we put four men on horses riding beside the carriage. Two men on horses on each side of the carriage, which made it pretty hard for anyone to get a clear shot at the prime minister."

"That's a great idea. After I get you and your men in their positions at the church, I'll see if I can make arrangements somehow to get four men on horses to cover the carriage for the trip to and from the church."

When they arrived at the church, Indian found the church was unlocked, and he was soon able to show the men where he wanted each of them positioned inside the church during the wedding.

Indian said, "Sean, I want you to be up in the balcony at the very front of the church where you will be able to see everything below you. I want your men to keep from allowing anyone else up there. You may not be able to see the very front of the church where the wedding ceremony will be taking place, but Rocky and I will be there, so we should be able to cover that area all right."

After Indian was sure each of the men knew where they were to be positioned, they all traveled back to the Sterlings' house. When they returned to the Sterlings', Indian told the men where he wanted them to take up positions outside the house before the wedding party left for the church.

Rocky had been busy telling the other three men where they were to be positioned before and after the wedding. After Indian finished positioning the three men outside for security, he and Sean went inside the house to find Rocky. They soon found Rocky in the library talking to Mr. Sterling about what measures they were taking to keep Joan safe during her wedding.

Indian said, "Rocky, Sean has a good idea of a way to keep the wedding party safe on the trip to the church and back. Sean told me he used this idea when he was in charge of security when the prime minister of England visited Dublin. Sean, why don't you tell them?"

Sean said, "Well, what we did was to have two men on horses on each side of his carriage while he traveled on the streets through Dublin."

Indian added, "I think that's a very good idea to keep Joan safe going and coming from the church. Rocky, I wonder if your father-in-law's security chief could let us have four of his men to help us protect the bride."

Rocky replied, "I'm sure he could get us four men. We would have to pay them, and I think his men have four white horses they could use."

John Sterling said, "I would be happy to pay for all the men and horses and whatever else you need to help keep Joan safe."

Rocky said, "I'll telephone Chuck Carson and ask him if he could provide us with four men and their horses to help with the security."

John showed Rocky where the telephone was in the library, and Rocky called Colonel Chuck Carson. Chuck told him he would contact four of his men and have them come to help provide security for the wedding, and they would be riding four white horses. He would have them at the Sterlings' house by noon. Rocky told him that Mr. Sterling would pay him for their services.

Indian said, "Well, I don't know of anything else we can do to provide any better security for Joan at the wedding."

Rocky said, "No, I don't know anything else we can do either." John said, "I have rented a special white wedding carriage with four white horses for their wedding. So the four men on white horses beside the carriage should provide quite a scene on the streets of New York."

Rocky said, "It should be some wedding procession."

Indian added, "We may be starting a whole new trend for weddings in New York with this wedding procession."

John said, "I'm not sure Joan will be happy about having a story about her wedding ending up in newspaper."

Then John showed then a picture on the front page of the newspaper with Patricia Sterling's picture wearing the fire chief's helmet, with headlines reading, "New York City's First Woman Fireman."

The story told all about lightning striking the tent for Joan Sterling's reception in her father's back garden and how Mrs. Sterling aided the fire department putting out the fire.

Indian said, "I think Mrs. Sterling looks charming in her fire helmet."

John said, "I do too. She looked very pretty."

At noon, the four horsemen arrived at the Sterlings' home riding their four white horses. All four of the horsemen were wearing white dress military-style uniforms and made quite a sight to see. By twelvefifteen, the white wedding carriage arrived with its four white horses. The driver and a footman were dressed in black uniforms. Everything was now ready for the drive to the church and back.

So far, none of the security men had seen anything that was of any concern for Joan's safety. At twelve forty-five, the groom, Robert Smiley, and his three attendants, Indian Leader, Rocky Stone, and Michael Sterling, left in their carriage for the church. At one o'clock, the bride, Joan Sterling, and her three attendants, Serene Leader, Latesha Stone, and Shannon Sterling, left in the wedding carriage for the church.

When the wedding carriage left the Sterling house, the four security men on their white horses joined the wedding carriage with two of the security men on their white horses on each side of the carriage.

As the traveled through the streets of New York, the other traffic had to pull over to the side of the street to allow the wedding carriage and its security men on horses to pass by. Soon, all the wedding party had reached the church, and the security men on their horses positioned themselves, providing a screen from the carriage to the church for the bride and her attendants to have safe passages into the church.

20

AT THE CHURCH

Short time after the wedding party arrived at the church, Joan's parents, John and Patricia Sterling, and Senator Wagner arrived at the church in their carriage. Everyone from the family was now at the church.

At the entrance to the church, on the left side of the foyer, was a door with a paper sign reading "Groom" and on the right side of the foyer was a paper sign on the door reading "Bride."

When John Sterling saw the signs on the doors, he went into the one for the groom and said, "I see the church wants to send a message to our groom.

Michael said, "What's that, Father?" "It says the bride is always right."

Everyone but Robert laughed. He wasn't so sure it was so funny.

Senator Wagner was seated in the second row on the left side of the church, and after a few minutes passed, his former aide, Larry Larson, came up to the senator and said, "Senator Wagner, may I sit down and talk with you, sir?"

Senator Wagner replied, "Yes, I guess you can, considering all the years you've worked for me."

"Sir, I'm so sorry for what I said about your family. I guess I just shouldn't drink. It causes me to not be myself."

"Son, you're not the only person I've known in my life who's has had that kind of a problem. So just sit here with me until after my granddaughter's wedding is over, and we'll go back to the house and we can talk things over, OK?"

"Yes, sir, thank you, sir."

Robert's parents, Tom and White Dove Smiley, were shown to their seats. In a few minutes, the church was full of people.

The Harbor policemen working as security for the wedding had been in their places long before the guests started arriving at the church. Sean was in his place in the church at the very front of the balcony where he had a clear view of the entire church floor.

A few minutes before two o'clock, John Sterling said, "Well, gentlemen, I guess it's time I leave you and get ready to bring Robert's bride down the aisle to him. Good luck, everyone. Let's hope this wedding goes off without any problem."

Indian replied, "I'm really going to be happy if it does." Rocky said, "Me too."

John left the groom's room to go over to the bride's room. He knocked on the door, and Serene opened the door.

She said, "Come in, Father of the Bride." John asked, "So how is our bride doing?" Joan replied, "Nervous!"

John said, "Well, you can call the whole thing off."

"Father, I'm not calling off my wedding. I've been waiting a long time to finally get married."

"OK, then. The wedding's on." John said, "All you ladies look wonderful."

They all said, "Thank you."

John asked, "Patricia, are you about ready to get this wedding started?"

"Yes, dear. I am."

They heard the music playing, and then came a knock on the door, and the usher said, "Mrs. Sterling, they're ready for you."

"OK, let's go."

Before she left the room, she gave Joan a hug and a kiss. The usher took Patricia's arm and walked her to her pew. Patricia took her place in front of the pew her father was sitting in and was surprised to see Larry Larson sitting next to her father.

A very few minutes passed and the wedding march began.

Indian said, "OK, Robert, it's time for us to go."

Michael opened the door and began walking down the aisle with Rocky following him, then Indian, and then Robert. They were now all in their places.

The music continued. Shannon was the first one to come down the aisle, followed by Latesha, and then Serene. Then, everyone in the church stood up and turned to watch Joan and her father come down the aisle. She made a beautiful bride, and her grown was a masterpiece.

Soon, Joan and her father arrived at the front of the church, and the minister said, "We are gathered here today to join these two people in holy matrimony. Who gives this woman in marriage?"

John replied, "Her mother and me."

John then gave Joan a kiss and turned to go to sit next to Patricia.

The minister then said, "Is anyone present who gives any just reason why these two people should not be married?"

The minister waited for a second before going on with the ceremony, not expecting anyone to say anything. Just as he started to go on with the ceremony, a man in the fourth row stood up.

He said, "I'm never letting this young woman marry no Indian and having a bunch of half-breed kids."

Then the man reached inside his coat and pulled out a gun.

Serene saw what he did and pulled Joan down, and Robert turned toward Joan when the shot was fired. Larry Larson had pulled Senator Wagner over in his seat. Sean fired one shot and hit the man. Indian and Rocky, with their guns drawn, ran toward the shooter, and by the time they reached the man, he had fallen down between the pews. Indian grabbed the man's gun out of his hand, as Rocky put his foot on the man's head, holding him down on the floor.

People began running out of the church as the security men outside rushed in and stopped anyone from leaving the church. They had no idea who fired shots in the church. They were looking for anyone who might have a gun.

Indian yelled at the security men and said, "There was only one shooter. He's been shot and is down on the floor between the pews here."

Two of them made their way up to Rocky, who had continued to hold the man down. Rocky took his foot off the man's head, and the two security men picked him up and carried him to the entrance of the church and took him into the groom's room. They found the man had been hit in the chest, and they got some bandages and were working trying to stop the bleeding.

In the meantime, Indian and Rocky went back to the front of the church to see if Joan was all right. She was, but Robert was sitting on the floor and holding his left shoulder. Indian could see blood flowing from his wound. His mother and father were there trying to help him.

Indian said, "Someone, get the doctor we have waiting in the basement in case Joan was hurt."

One of the church staff told Indian he would go and bring the doctor upstairs.

Indian asked, "Robert, where did you get hit?"

Robert replied, "It's my left shoulder. I don't think it's too bad, but it hurts like hell."

A few minutes later, the church worker and the doctor came to where Robert was sitting, and the doctor took a quick look at Robert's shoulder and said, "We need to get him somewhere where he can be lying down, and let me get that bullet out and get him stitched up. We need to stop that bleeding."

The minister said, "I have a daybed in my office. You can take him in there."

The doctor asked, "Do you think you can walk?" Robert replied, "I think so."

Robert stood up, and Indian thought he looked like he was going to fall, so Indian grabbed him and helped to hold him up on his left side.

Rocky went to his right side and was helping him to stand. Then they started walking slowly, following the minister to his office. Slowly, they made their way into the minister's office, with all the wedding party and Robert's parents following them into the office. Indian and Rocky helped Robert sit down on the daybed, and Indian started taking off his bloodstained jacket. Serene came over and began unsnapping the snaps on his Western dress shirt.

The doctor said, "I need someone to get me some warm water and some clean towels."

The minister said, "I'll have someone get those for you, Doctor." The minister left the room to get the warm water and towels.

Indian and Serene helped take Robert's shirt off and laid it off on a table.

The doctor said, "Can you help him to lie down on the bed now? I need to take a good look at that wound."

Indian and Rocky slowly laid Robert down on the daybed with his long legs hanging over the end of the daybed.

Indian said, "It's not good trying to lay you down on such a short little bed when you're six foot seven."

Rocky got a chair and put a big soft pillow on the chair, and Indian and Rocky raised his legs up and placed them on the pillow. Robert's mother, White Dove, stood at top of Robert's head and gently touched his forehead, letting him know she was with him. Robert smiled at his mother through his pain to let her know he knew she was there.

The doctor asked, "Can anyone of you help me while I'm taking the bullet out of his shoulder?"

Serene said, "I can help you, Doctor." "Good."

The doctor opened his bag and took out two pairs of rubber gloves, gave a pair to Serene, and put on the other pair. Serene put her gloves on.

Then the doctor said, "Robert, if you think you can make it all right, we can do this here, but it would be better if we could take you to the hospital. There, we could put you to sleep, and you wouldn't feel the pain that you're going to feel here. I can give you a shot for the pain before we begin, if you want me to do it here. It will help some, but it would be much better if we could do it at the hospital. What do you want me to do?"

Robert said, "I want you to take the bullet out and get me stitched up so we can finish our wedding."

"OK, you're the doctor. No, I guess I'm the doctor. We'll get started, and I'll do it as easy as possible for you."

The minister and one of the church workers came back in the office with a large pan of warm water and lots of towels. The doctor took out a syringe and a bottle of some kind of painkiller and filled the syringe and gave Robert a shot in his shoulder, just above the bullet wound.

Then the doctor said, "If you're ready, young woman, we'll get started. What's your name?"

Serene answered, "Serene."

"OK, Serene, dip one of those towels into the warm water and clean off as much of the blood as you can around the wound."

Serene took one of the towels and began washing the blood away from the wound. It was now much easier to see where the bullet had entered Robert's shoulder. The doctor then took a small pair of tweezers and tried to reach the bullet, but it was too deep in the shoulder muscle for him to reach with his tweezers. The doctor had laid out cotton swabs before he had started trying to remove the bullet. He asked Serene to take the swabs and keep wiping away the blood so he could see. Then the doctor took a small scalpel and made an incision into the skin where the bullet had entered Robert's shoulder, opening the area up more, and blood begin flowing harder.

The doctor said, "Serene, keep wiping the blood away from the area of the incision."

Serene kept working, wiping away the blood, and the doctor said, "OK, Serene, let me try to reach that bullet again."

Serene took the swab away, and the doctor took his tweezers and a small probe and lifted up one end of the spent bullet. Then he managed to grasp the bullet with the tweezers and pulled it out of Robert's shoulder.

Serene kept wiping away the blood, and the doctor took some kind of fluid and cleaned the whole area of the wound. This made Robert groan with pain.

The doctor said, "Hang on, son, we're just about through. We'll have you stitched up in just a few more minutes. Serene, can you thread one of those needles for me while I'm changing my gloves?"

"Yes, Doctor."

Serene made one more wipe with one of the swabs and put it into the wastebasket, where she had been putting the used towels and swabs before.

Serene picked up one of the needles the doctor had laid out before he began the operation and threaded the needle with the thread he had lying there.

The doctor said, "Thank you, Serene. Let's get Robert sewed up so he can finish his wedding vows."

It took the doctor only a few more minutes to get the wound sewn up, and he said, "OK, Robert, you're going to be all right now. Before you get dressed, I'm going to give you one more shot for your pain, which should help you get through your wedding. I've also given Serene several pain pills for you, so we can try to keep you out of as much pain as we possibly can. It's going to take a few weeks before you'll be completely healed, but then, you should be just as strong as you ever were."

White Dove had continued to stroke his forehead all through the surgery to try to keep him calm.

Robert said as he was sitting up, "Thank you, Doctor, for getting that bullet out and, Mom, thanks for being here for me."

The doctor said, "I want to thank my wonderful nurse. I couldn't have done it without you, Serene. Thank you so much."

Joan came to Serene and said, "Thank you for helping. I could have never done that."

Serene said, "It comes from living in the West. You learn to do whatever needs to be done."

Indian said, "Yes, she had experience. She helped get a bullet out of me once.

The doctor said, "I better take a look at the other man who was shot to see what I can do for him."

The minister said, "I'll take you to where he is."

The two of them left to see what the doctor could do for the shooter's wound.

A few minutes later, the minister returned and said, "The doctor said they would have to take the shooter to the hospital to operate on him. He couldn't do the surgery here. He didn't have enough equipment. Robert, do you think you can go on with the wedding ceremony?"

"I think so."

Joan asked, "Are you sure you can do it, my love?"

Robert said, "We better get married before anything else happens." The minister said, "I'll go make an announcement to the folks who are left in the church and let them know that we'll finish the ceremony in a few minutes."

Indian had Robert's shirt and said, "I'll see if I can wash some of the blood off the shirt."

Serene looked at the shirt and said, "Indian, the blood is dry. I think it would be better if Robert just wore it as it is instead of getting it wet. I think it would be more comfortable with the bloodstain on it than to wear a wet shirt."

"OK, Serene. I think you're right. How about his jacket?" Serene looked at the jacket and said, "It's got some blood on it, but I don't think it looks too bad."

Joan looked at Robert's jacket and said, "Let's not try to do anything with it. I don't know how it may look in our wedding pictures, but it will have to do."

Indian and Rocky helped Robert get his shirt and jacket on. Then they helped him back out to the front of the church, and Indian said, "Maybe we should have you sit in a chair to finish your wedding ceremony."

Robert replied, "That probably would be a good idea, but no, I'll make it through the ceremony standing."

The minister asked the rest of the wedding party to get back in their positions so they could finish the ceremony. Quickly, everyone was back in their places, and the minister picked up the ceremony where he had left off.

He certainly didn't want to ask again if anyone had any objections to Robert and Joan getting married.

The ceremony was soon over, and the minister said, "You may kiss the bride."

Robert leaned down to kiss Joan; he gave her a nice kiss, and then when he was straightening back up, he began to wobble. Indian saw it and thought he was going to fall. He quickly caught his right arm and steadied him.

The minister said, "Ladies and gentlemen, may I introduce you to Mr. and Mrs. Robert Smiley."

The people who were still left in the church applauded them. Robert and Joan had turned around to face the audience, and then with Joan and Indian's help for Robert, they began walking out of the church to their waiting white wedding carriage with its team of four white horses.

By the time they got to the carriage, Rocky had caught up with them, and he and Indian got Robert and Joan into the carriage. The four security guards, on their white horses, were waiting and ready to take the couple back to the Sterlings' house. The rest of the wedding party got into their carriages and would be following right behind the wedding carriage.

Away they went, traveling through the New York streets at a very fast clip, and they were soon at the Sterlings' home. Joan and Robert waited in their carriage until the carriage with Indian and Rocky and Michael arrived.

They three of them helped Rocky get out of the carriage and into the house, and the rest of the wedding party arrived soon after them. Robert said, "Joan, you can't be kissing me until I get my strength back. You saw what almost happened to me at the church.

I almost passed out from your kiss."

Indian said, "I thought you were hurting, but no, you can still give people a bad time, I see."

Joan said, "Yeah, I thought you were serious about me not kissing you.

"Well, I was, you saw what happened at the church. I almost fell all the way to the floor after that last kiss and would have if Indian hadn't caught me."

"Too bad, I plan on kissing you a lot while you're in your weakened condition."

Indian and Rocky took Robert into the library to let him sit down while Joan got him a clean shirt and another jacket to wear for their reception.

A few minutes later, Joan came back with a clean Western shirt and another Western jacket. Indian and Rocky helped Robert take off his bloody jacket and shirt. Then they helped him put on the shirt and jacket that Joan had brought him to wear. Next, they helped Robert into the reception tent and got him into a chair at the head table, and Joan sat down next to him.

All the family began coming by to congratulate them on their wedding, followed by the guests who had remained for the wedding ceremony and the reception.

Indian and Rocky left to talk with Sean to see if he was holding up all right after shooting the assailant that shot Robert. The three of them went into the library to discuss the events of the shooting.

When they were in the library, Indian said, "Sean, did you have a clear view of the whole main floor of the church from your position in the church balcony?"

"I certainly did."

"Sean, I've been playing back in my mind all the events of the shooting, and one thing that I think I saw was before the shooter took out his gun. I'd swear I saw Senator Wagner's aide, Larry Larson, push the senator down on the pew before the man fired a shot. Do you remember anything like that?"

"I don't know. Everything happened so fast, I'm not sure."

Rocky said, "The only thing I remember was looking at the man who started talking and then he pulled his gun. I remember thinking, who was this guy and how did he get an invitation to the wedding?"

Indian said, "Now that's a very good question. He certainly didn't dress like all the other men at the wedding, that's for sure."

Sean added, "No, he didn't. While you were in with Robert being treated by the doctor, I telephoned the police and reported the shooting, and they were going to send someone to the hospital to check on the guy to see if they knew who he was."

Indian said, "Good thinking, Sean."

Rocky asked, "Sean, who did you talk to at the police department?" "When I told them who I was, they put me through to a Captain Troy McDonald."

Indian asked, "Do you think they may have had time to send someone to the hospital to check on the guy?"

"I don't know, but I could call Captain McDonald back and ask him."

Rocky said, "Why don't you do that, Sean?"

Sean went over to the desk and telephoned the police department and got Captain McDonald and asked if they had time to check on their shooter.

The captain told Sean they did and said the man's name was Tony Capon and that they had warrants out for his arrest for armed robbery, attempted murder, assault, and resisting arrest. The captain told Sean they were assigning two men to his room until he was well enough to be taken into custody. When Sean finished his conversation with the captain, he told Indian and Rocky what he found out about their shooter.

Indian said, "Let's see if we can find the senator's aide, Larry Larson.

I'm pretty sure when the guy stood up and started talking, Larry pushed the senator down on the pew before the shooter had his gun out. Like he knew what was going to happen."

They found Larry talking to Robert and telling him how bad he felt about him getting shot. Indian asked Larry to come with him. They had some questions about the shooting and needed his help.

Larry followed Indian and Rocky into the library, and when they got there, Indian said, "You may have saved the senator's life by pushing him down on his pew since you were sitting right in front of the shooter."

"I've been looking after the senator a long time, it's what I do." Indian asked, "One thing that bothers us is when the man stood up and started shouting, you pushed the senator down. What made you do that?"

"What do you mean asking a question like that? I told you I've been looking after the senator for a long time. I didn't want him to get hurt."

Indian asked again, "We understand that you didn't want the senator to get hurt, but has something like that happened before that you knew the man was going to pull out a gun and fire it?"

"No, I'm glad to say that in all the time I've worked for the senator, no one ever took out a gun and fired it."

Indian didn't back off his with questioning and said, "Maybe you knew someone was going to try and kill either the bride or the groom, did you?"

"What are you trying to say, that I had something to do with the man who fired the shot?"

Indian fired back, "Did you?"

"How would I know something like that? I know that a lot of people weren't happy about the senator's granddaughter marrying an Indian, but I never thought anyone would try to shoot him."

"I don't know about what you're telling me. What about you, Larry? I know last night you were very upset about Joan marrying an Indian. Maybe you hired someone to kill either Joan or Robert, did you?"

"No, I didn't hire someone to shoot anyone."

Indian continued, "You sounded mad enough last night to do exactly that. If you didn't do it, who did hire him? I know you knew someone was going to try to kill one of them. That's the reason you pushed the senator down, wasn't it, Larry?"

Larry began to tremble, and Indian and Rocky didn't know which way he was going to react, exploding or crying. Indian had questioned enough men in his life that he understood that one of these things was going to happen very soon. So Indian never said another word until he could see which Larry would do. The three of them sat there for maybe five very long minutes before Indian could see tears forming in his eyes.

Then Indian said, "Larry, why don't you do all of us a favor and just tell us what you know about the man who shot Robert?"

Now tears were falling down Larry's face, and he said, "The don of the New York Mafia made me do it."

Indian said, "What did he make you do, Larry?"

"He made me get him an invitation for the wedding sent to the man, the man who fired a shot and hit Robert."

"How did he get you two get an invitation for the man to attend the wedding, Larry?"

"He threatened to expose me to the senator." "How could he do that?"

"I owed the bookies lots of money for gambling and for the services of their women, and he said he would give me back all my markers and they would all be marked paid and they wouldn't tell the senator about my problem with gambling and about the women."

"Who is this don of the New York Mafia?" "His name is Don San Marco."

"Are you sure that's his name?"

"I'm very sure. They took me to meet him personally."

"I saw in the newspaper sometime ago that he had been found dead and was killed by some other New York gangsters."

"I was told that Don San Marco was his father and that he was killed by you and not by some New York gang, and he was going to have your best friend, Robert Smiley, killed to get even with you for killing his father."

"You should know that's not true. I never killed his father."

"I can tell you that's not going to make any difference to them. They believe you did, and they're going to get even with you if it's the last thing they ever do."

Rocky who had been quiet during all this questioning said, "Friend, I would say that it's likely it will be the last thing they will ever do if they try to hurt Indian."

Indian said, "I think it best if you leave right now. We'll tell the senator you decided it would be best if you left his employment because the shooting at the church was just too much for you. If you do, we won't tell the senator about you having anything to do with getting Robert shot. Is that agreeable with you, Larry?"

"OK, it is. I'm sorry your friend Robert was hurt." Larry got up from the couch and left.

Indian and Rocky watched as he went out the front door.

They went back into the library, and Rocky said, "What do you think about that, Don San Marco having a son by the same name?" "I hate to think about it. I thought we were through with Mafia.

This time, I guess we have to kill a bunch of them to put across the idea that you don't mess with the New York Harbor Police."

21

THE RECEPTION

Robert and Joan were seated at the head table along with Indian and Serene, Rocky and Latesha, and Michael and Shannon. The bride and groom's parents and Senator Wagner were seated at an adjoining table next to them. The rest of the guests were seated at tables all around the tent.

After everyone was finally seated, the waiters began filling their glasses with champagne.

Indian stood up and said, "You know, as the best man at my best friend's wedding, I'm obligated to say something nice about my friend. However, I'm going to tell you the truth."

Indian waited for the crowd's reaction, which was quiet laughter. "Folks, the truth is Robert is the best man I have ever met in my life. He's loyal, friendly, and always willing to help you out. That's kind of like saying your best friend is your favorite dog." Again, laughter from the audience.

"I have known Robert since we were five years old and growing up on the Cherokee Indian reservation in Oklahoma Territory. We went to school together there. He was always the smartest kid in class all through our school years. I think it pays to have two smart teachers as your parents.

We got into fights together, and he always came through for me, but he always waited to see if I could handle four or five guys all by myself before he came to my rescue. He would say, 'Well, I never thought you'd need any help with just four or five guys.'"

More laughter from the audience.

"There's one thing for sure: Joan has picked one of the best men in the world for her husband. I know he will always be there for her, no matter what happens. I do have to say though, normally, where I come from, you don't get shot for marrying the girl, it's when you don't."

More laughter from the audience.

"So let's all raise our glasses and toast the new bride and groom, Mr. and Mrs. Robert Smiley." Indian raised his glass and took a small sip and said, "Good luck to my best friend. Robert, may you always be happy. Congratulations, my friend."

There was applause from the audience as Indian sat down, and Serene got up.

Serene began, "Well, I don't know how to follow what my husband had to say about his best friend. In the first place, I never knew my husband was that funny."

This drew laughter from the audience.

"Joan and I haven't known each other quite as long as Indian and Robert. We met when we were about twelve years old. You know, of course, after that age, women don't like to spend a lot of time talking about how old they are. We went through several years of school together and continued to be together when we both went to Vassar, where we were joined by a third roommate, Latesha. So the three of us became very close friends.

"When Indian and I were married, Joan came to Kansas City to be my maid of honor and that's where she met Robert, who was Indian's best man.

"We girls know how each other think sometimes, and when she saw Robert and spent some time with him, I knew he was a goner. Joan was determined to have him as her husband."

This brought more laughter from the audience.

"Joan and her family have been part of my family almost all my life, and she is like the sister I never had. I love her dearly, and I know she will make Robert a very happy man. So would you please raise your glasses one more time and toast our bride and groom, Joan and Robert. May God truly bless them."

Everyone again took a sip of their champagne.

After Serene sat down, Robert said, "Folks, I want to say a few words, but I'm sorry that I don't feel well enough to stand up right now. I just wanted to say thank you to all of you for coming to our wedding, and I want you all to enjoy yourself with a lot of my father-in-law's champagne and the wonderful meal I know the staff has prepared for you. One thing I want to say about what my best friend had to say about me being the smartest kid in school: frankly, I didn't have a lot of competition for that honor."

People laughed at what Robert said.

"I'm talking to everyone right now because I'm afraid I'm going to have to say good night because my pain medication is beginning to wear off, and I'm beginning to have a lot of pain with my shoulder now. This is not exactly the way I thought I would be feeling on my wedding night, but again, thank you for joining us for our wedding. I'm sure it's one wedding you've attended that is unlike any one you've ever attended before, and I'm sure you will always remember our wedding."

Indian said, "Robert, are you ready to go to your room?"

"I'm not ready, but I have to go. My pain is too much right now." Indian and Rocky each got on one side of Robert and began helping him up from his chair and slowly guided him through the tent into the house and headed him upstairs to his bedroom. Joan, Serene, and Latesha followed right behind them.

When they arrived at Robert's room, Serene said, "Robert, the doctor gave me some pain pills for you. I'll get you some water, and you can take a couple of them to see if they will ease your pain some."

"OK, Serene. I'll be glad to take them as soon as you can get me some water."

Joan went with Serene to show her where Robert's bathroom was, and they got a glass, filled it with water, and brought it back to Robert where Serene gave him two of the pain pills. Robert took the glass and quickly took the pain pills.

Indian said, "We'll help you get undressed so you can get in your bed."

Rocky said, "Wow, Robert, that's the biggest bed I ever saw in my life."

Robert answered, "It's probably unlike any other bed in New York. Joan's dad had it made for me right after I moved in with them. Mr. Sterling said to me after I was here a few nights, 'How are you able to sleep in the bed we have in your room?' I told him I had never slept in the bed. I took off the blankets and pillows and slept on the floor. He told me that no guest in his house was going to have to sleep on the floor, so he had some man measure how tall I was and then he made my bed to fit me. It was the first time I ever had a bed to sleep on. It was wonderful."

Indian begin taking off Robert's boots and said, "Robert, you need to stop talking and let us get you into bed. Girls, why don't you step out in the hallway and let Rocky and I get Robert into bed."

Joan, Serene, and Latesha left the bedroom and stepped out in the hallway.

Serene said, "I don't think this was what you had planned for your wedding night, Joan. I'm sorry."

Joan replied, "Well, at least, I finally got married in June, even if it was the last day of June, so I'm still a June bride."

Latesha said, "There will be other nights in your life with Robert. At least, neither one of you were killed. If you had been shot instead of hitting Robert in the shoulder, that bullet would have probably hit you in the chest."

Joan said, "You're right, and I need to thank Serene for pulling me down to the floor and keeping me from being shot."

"Indian told me if there was any trouble that I was to push you down on the floor."

Just as Serene finished saying that, Robert's bedroom door opened, and Rocky said, "You girls can come back in now. We've got Robert in bed."

The girls returned to Robert's room and saw Robert in his huge bed, looking like he might be doing a little bit better.

Indian said, "Joan, I think you can handle everything now, so we will say good night and see you in a few days to see how Robert and you are doing."

Serene said, "Joan, here are some more of the pain pills. You shouldn't give him any more for at least four hours, then you can give him two more pain pills every four hours as long as he needs them for his pain."

Then Serene went over to Robert's bed and leaned over and gave Robert a kiss on his cheek.

Next, Latesha did the same and said, "I hope you recover quickly, Robert."

Indian and Rocky came back up next to his bed, and Indian said, "I hope you can get to feeling better real soon, partner. I love you, and I'm so sorry we couldn't have done a better job of protecting you."

Robert said, "Thank you both. You saved us from something that could have been much worse."

Rocky said, "Well, we are truly sorry, we just couldn't keep you from getting hurt, Robert. We do hope you get some rest and recover quickly. Good night, Robert."

They all gave Joan a hug and a kiss and left Robert's bedroom. On the way out of the house, they stopped to tell Sean to let the Harbor police officers go home since they didn't think there would be any more problems now and to thank them so much for their help.

After all the people left Robert's room, he said, "Joan, I'm so sorry I got shot and ruined our wedding night."

"Oh, Robert, I so sorry you were shot, but it wasn't your fault! You got shot trying to protect me. I love you so much, and we'll have lots more nights together."

"Joan, my pain pills are helping with my pain and maybe some rest will help me recover. Good night, Joan. I love you so much, and I'm glad we were at least able to finally get married."

Joan replied, "Yes, my darling. We finally were able to get married, and I look forward to many more wedding nights after you recover from your wound. I love you so much."

The following morning, before seven o'clock, the telephone was ringing at Indian and Serene's suite at the Waldorf, and Serene answered the telephone and sleepily said, "Hello."

Rocky said, "Serene, it's Rocky. I need to talk to Indian." "OK, Rocky."

Serene handed the telephone to Indian and said, "Indian, it's Rocky."

Indian took the telephone and said, "Good morning, Rocky. What's going on?"

"I'm sorry to call you so early, but I just got a call from the New York City Police Department who advised me that in spite of having two police officers outside the room of the man who shot Robert, someone cut the shooter's throat last night."

Indian replied, "Sounds like the Mafia is trying to clean up all their tracks so no one knows they were involved in Robert's shooting. You know what that means, Rocky? Larry Larson is next on their list. We need to get to his place as soon as we can."

"I agree, Indian. How soon can you be ready if I come by and pick you up?"

"I'll be ready whenever you get here."

"I'm ready to go after I telephone Senator Wagner and get Larry's address."

"Good, I'll be waiting outside of the hotel for you."

Indian got out of bed, took a quick shower, shaved, dressed, and was down waiting for Rocky in fifteen minutes. He had been waiting less than five minutes when Rocky arrived, driving the carriage himself.

Rocky said, "Good morning, Indian, after I got the address for Larry Larson, I telephoned Captain Troy McDonald and asked him how someone got into Tony Capon's hospital room since they had two police officers guarding the room. The captain told me they let a doctor in his room. They checked his ID, and he was wearing the same green uniform they wear in surgery. The man told them he was the doctor who operated on Tony and just wanted to see how he was doing.

"They said after he came out of the room, they asked how his patient was doing, and they said he told them if he makes it through the night, he should be all right. A couple of hours passed before a nurse came to check on the patient again. She immediately came running out of the room and said someone had cut the patient's throat. The officers went in the room and saw that, indeed, his throat had been cut and blocked the room so the room could be examined for any clues. They checked on the doctor whose name the killer had on his ID and found the doctor was in the operating room with eight other doctors and nurses at that time the killer came into the room. The doctor checked, and yes, his billfold was missing from the doctor's dressing room."

Indian said, "We better get to Larry's apartment in a hurry before he's the next victim of this killer."

When they pulled up in front of the building where Larry's apartment was, there was a carriage with a driver waiting at the curb. When Rocky stopped their carriage, Indian said, "Rocky, why don't you stay in the carriage and wait to see if someone comes rushing out of the building in a hurry and gets into that carriage, you may have to follow them because I have a feeling we may be too late to save Larry."

Indian got out of the carriage and entered the building and started up the stairs as some man came running down. The man bumped into him, and before he recovered, the man was out the door. Indian then ran up the stairs and found Larry's apartment number on the first door at the head of the stairs. Indian knocked on the door, but no one answered the door. Then Indian pounded on the door as hard as he could, but still no answer.

Indian went down the stairs and knocked on a door; it took a few minutes before an older lady answered the door, and Indian asked, "Ma'am, are you the landlady?"

"Yes, I am. I own the building. What can I do for you?"

"My name is Indian Leader, and I'm afraid something has happened to one of your tenants, Larry Larson. I knocked on his door, and no one answers the door."

She said, "Larry has probably gone to Washington with Senator Wagner. He's often gone."

"Ma'am, I know he's home because he was with me yesterday, along with Senator Wagner, and they weren't planning on going back to

Washington until next week. I'm afraid something may have happened to him."

"Well, if you're sure. I'll get my key, and we can go check on him to be sure he's all right. He's such a nice young man."

"Yes, ma'am."

"I'll be right back."

She was gone for only a couple of minutes before she returned with a key. She started up the stairs with Indian following right behind her. When they arrived at Larry's door, she knocked on the door and waited to see if he would answer the door.

When he didn't answer the door right away, Indian said, "I'm really afraid that something has happened to him, ma'am, I think you should open the door to see if we can help him."

"OK, if you think it's best to do that." "Yes, ma'am, I do think it's for the best."

The landlady put the key in the door and unlocked the door.

She slowly opened the door, saying, "Larry, are you OK?"

No answer, so she went on inside the apartment with Indian following behind her; she went past the living room and into the bedroom. She saw Larry lying on his bed with blood all over his throat area and down his chest, lying there with his eyes wide open. When she saw him, she said, "Oh my gosh, Larry's dead.

Someone has cut his throat."

Indian walked over to where Larry's body was lying, and he could see she was correct, his throat had been cut.

Indian said, "Ma'am, we need to telephone the police and report this murder."

"Yes, we must do that. I know whoever killed him cut his throat. That's what a lot of the killers do in those detective stories I read. It certainly looks like an awful way to die."

Indian replied, "Yes, ma'am, it is. Don't touch anything in here and lock the room back up until the police get here.

They went back downstairs, and Indian asked the landlady if she would like him to talk to the police for her.

She said, "Yes, I would."

Indian telephoned the police and reported the murder and gave the police the address of the victim. The landlady asked him if he would like to sit down and wait for the police to come. Indian agreed; he would wait for the police, but first, he would check to see if his friend was still waiting for him in their carriage. Indian went to the front window and looked out and saw that Rocky was gone. When Indian went into the house, Rocky saw the man come rushing out of the house and jump in the carriage parked in front of his carriage. Then the driver immediately took off, so Rocky began to follow them.

Rocky let the other carriage get ahead a little way as he began to follow it and continued to follow it. Whenever it turned on a street, he also turned, always staying a little way behind it.

The driver of the other carriage made several turns on several streets, but Rocky was able to keep his carriage in sight. They traveled down First Street for a long way, and then the carriage finally turned on Central Park Avenue. Rocky slowed down and went slowly by Central Park Avenue.

Then as soon as his carriage passed Central Park Avenue, he pulled the carriage up to the curb. He tied the reins of his horses and walked back to look down Central Park Avenue to see what was happening. He saw the carriage come to a stop, and the man that had come out of Larry Larson's apartment building got out of the carriage.

The man looked both ways and walked up the stairs of one of the buildings on the street. The man stood there for a little while and looked up and down the street again, and then he walked back down the stairs and went over to the house next door. When the man got to the door of this house, he opened the door and went inside.

Rocky said to himself, "That son of a gun doesn't trust anyone." After Rocky was sure the man was going to stay inside the house, he walked down the street and wrote down the address of the house, 208 Central Park Avenue. After he did that, he walked back to his carriage and began making his way back to where he had left Indian at Larry Larson's apartment. By the time Rocky made it back to the apartment, the police were there and had been busy writing up the information on the murder of Larry Larson.

The police took down all the information they could from Indian about what he knew about the murder and told him he could go. Indian walked out of the house only a few minutes after Rocky arrived with the carriage; he got into the carriage, and Rocky drove away from the apartment.

After they had driven a little way, Rocky said, "I think I found the headquarters of the Mafia. I followed the carriage the man who left the apartment got in, and I think I found the address of the people we're looking for. The guy thought he was pretty smart because when he got out of the carriage, he looked both ways and went up the steps at 206 Central Park Avenue. He stood at the door, looked around again, didn't see anyone and went back down the stairs and then went to 208 Central Park Avenue, opened the door, and went in."

"Well, Rocky, we're dealing with a professional killer, and it pays him to be very careful."

"Yes, we are, so what are we professional law enforcement officers going to do now?"

"I would suggest we set up a watch on this house to be sure we have the right house. If it is, we'll need to get as many of the Mafia leaders, especially Don San Marco, and shoot them down like the mad dogs they are. I want to send a message to the head of the Mafia in Sicily, so they don't mess with the Harbor Police Department ever again."

"Indian, how do you suggest we do that?"

"Well, we're going to have to have help. We can't do it all by ourselves. We also don't want to involve any of the men from the Harbor police, except maybe Sean. I don't think the rest of the officers would understand us being judge, jury, and the hangman. It might give them the idea that doing this is all right, and they might begin doing it with every petty lawbreaker. However, we do need to have two men on every eight-hour shift. Do you have any idea where we can get some more men?"

"I think I do. I'll contact Colonel Chuck Carson and see if we can get three men from him."

"Great idea. That man might know something that could help us."

22

THE STAKEOUT

Then Rocky left to see about getting three men from Colonel Carson to help them with the stakeout.

Indian had told Rocky that he would stay and see if he could see anyone going in and out of 208 Central Park Avenue. Indian had to work hard to stay out of view of the house he was watching. He knew that dressed the way Rocky and he dressed in their Western clothes, they would soon be spotted.

Indian walked around, trying to find somewhere he could see the house without being seen from 208 Central Park Avenue. He spotted a For Rent sign on the house directly across the street at 209 Central Park Avenue.

Indian crossed the street, went inside, and found the manager's office on the first floor.

He knocked on the door, and a lady came to the door and asked, "May I help you?"

"Yes, ma'am. I wanted to ask about the apartment you have for rent?"

The lady said, "The apartment is on the second floor. It has two bedrooms, a combination living and dining area, a small kitchen, and a bathroom."

"May I take a look at the apartment?"

"Certainly you can. I'd be glad to show it to you. Just follow me up the stairs."

The landlady climbed the stairs, and when she got to the second floor, she went to an apartment at the front of the house, took out a key, and opened the door. Indian followed her inside the apartment, took a look around, went to the windows facing the street, and found this apartment looked directly into the front window of the house across the street. Indian thought, This couldn't be any better for our purpose. He asked her how much the rent was for the apartment.

She said, "As you probably know, everything in New York is very expensive. This apartment rents for two hundred dollars a month, and we require a one-year lease."

Indian said, "Ma'am, my associates and I are only going to be here on a project for a month, but your apartment is just what we need. Would you consider renting it to me if I gave you a thousand dollars for one month and paid it in advance?"

"Well, if you're sure you're only going to be here for one month, I guess I could do that for you."

"OK, ma'am, it's a deal."

Indian took out his billfold and counted out one thousand dollars in one hundred dollar bills.

The landlady said, "My name is Lucy Brown. What is your name, so I can write you a receipt for the month's rent?"

"Well, ma'am, my name is Indian Leader."

"Indian Leader, that's a very unusual name. I never heard of anyone whose first name was Indian."

"No, ma'am, I'm sure you didn't. My mother named me that because I was born in Indian Territory. Not too long after I was born, both of my parents were killed by Indians. Then some Cherokee Indians found me, and I got a ma and pa who were Cherokee Indians, and they took me in and raised me. They found my name in my mother's Bible, which was the only thing I had with me when they found me. They said they thought I was about three or four years old when they found me. They raised me, so they are the only parents I've ever had, and they love me like I was their own, and I love them."

"That's a very interesting story. Folks here in the east think all Indians out west are just savages and aren't real people or have any feelings at all." "Yes, ma'am, I know how people here feel about Indians, but they're wrong. They love and care for their family the same as the white people do here in New York, and they care about other members of the tribe too. They're all part of their family."

"Thank you for telling me about that. I'll get you a receipt for the month's rent and be right back. You can take a look around at the rest of the apartment while I'm gone."

Indian did look around the apartment and spent more time looking at the house across the street. Yes, sir, this apartment was perfect for their needs.

Lucy Brown came back with his receipt for a thousand dollars for one month and gave him two keys for the apartment. She told him if he needed anything to let her know.

Lucy said, "There's a back door that you can come in from the alley, if you want to. You don't have to come in by the front door, and there's a space for a carriage back there and a livery stable in the alley at the end of the block."

Indian said, "Thank you, ma'am. I'm glad you told me about that." "Indian, please just call me Lucy. You don't have to call me ma'am." "Sorry, ma'am, I mean, Lucy, it just my upbringing."

"Your ma did a fine job of bringing you up right and proper." "Thank you, ma'am, I mean, Lucy."

Lucy just smiled and said, "Thank you, Indian. You make me feel like a real lady."

She left, and Indian went downstairs and found the back door that made the apartment perfect. They could come and go without ever being on Central Park Avenue, using the back door. Indian walked back to where Rocky had left him and decided to wait there. He could still see the house they were going to be watching, but not nearly as well as he could from their new apartment.

Two hours later, Rocky returned and said, "How are you doing, and have you seen anyone go in or out of the house?"

"I'm doing OK, and no, I haven't seen anyone go in or out of the house, but I did rent us an upstairs apartment at 209 Central Park Avenue.

It's perfect, we can see anyone going in or out of the house, and we can see right in the front window inside the house in what looks like the living room. Also, we can go into the house from the alley, so we never have to be seen on Central Park Avenue."

"That sound great, Indian. How did you find it?"

"I started walking down Central Park Avenue and saw a For Rent sign and went over to the house. The landlady showed me the apartment and although she said she wanted two hundred dollars a month and a one-year lease to rent the apartment, I got her to rent it to me for a month for a thousand dollars. I think it will keep us from ever being seen by any of the Mafia, until we're ready for them to see us."

"That sounds good, Indian. I did pretty well too. I talked to Colonel Carson, and he's giving us three men for as long as we need them. He also got on the telephone and called someone at City Hall and found out who owns 208 Central Park Avenue. It's Don San Marco."

"Damn, Rocky, I can't believe we're still dealing with the same man who was supposed to have been killed."

"Well, it's not the same man. It's his son and the grandson of the big Mafia leader in Sicily. To change the deed to the property from his father to his name, this Don San Marco had to bring a copy of his father's will, a death certificate, and a copy of his birth certificate."

"I can't believe it."

"It's true. Colonel Carson also contacted the people who did the census last year and found the only people living in the apartment house are fifteen Italian men. No women and no families."

"Which means the only people living there are all Mafia." "Right, and we have our three men starting tomorrow morning.

We'll set up three shifts, starting at seven tomorrow morning, and if you want, you can take that shift or if you want the second shift, which starts at 3:00 p.m., you can have it."

"I've talked with Sean and he's willing to take the eleven to seven shift."

"OK, Rocky, I'll take the first shift, and you can have the second shift."

"Good! On the day shift, you'll be working with John Smith. I'll have Bobbie Thomas, and Sean will be with Tank Giles. Colonel Carson told me that's the way they set up stakeouts of suspected criminals in the past."

"Sounds good to me, Rocky, but I want to take you to see the apartment, so you can tell everyone where we will be working."

Indian got into Rocky's carriage, and Rocky drove to the alley, turned his horses into the alley behind Central Park Avenue and West First Street, and drove until Indian pointed to the back of the house and said, "That's the house. You can pull up right there."

Indian showed Rocky into the building, then they went up the stairs and to the apartment he had rented. Rocky looked around the apartment and took a look out the front window, and he could plainly see the house they would be watching and then he saw someone through the house's front window.

"Indian, you're right. You can certainly see anyone who enters or exits the house. Looking through their front window right now, I think I'm looking at Don San Marco."

Indian peered out the window and said, "Yeah, that guy looks like a younger Don San Marco, so I think you're right, that's got to be him."

Rocky looked at the rest of the apartment and said, "You're right, Indian. This is perfect for what we need. We've got tables and chairs, and we've got a bathroom, if we need it, and a couple of beds so one of the guys could lie down and rest for a while while the other one is watching the house. I think I need to bring some pencils and note paper so we can keep track of everyone who goes in or out of the house and the time they come and go. We may not know the men's names, but we can describe them and give each one of them some kind of name, so we know who comes and goes at the house."

"Great idea, Rocky. I want to know when the house has the most Mafia men inside because I want to hit them when we can do the most damage to their organization here in New York City."

"OK, I think we've got a plan. We might as well leave right now so I can organize the pencils and note paper."

"OK, Rocky. You can tell John Smith I'll be here tomorrow a little before seven and ask him to bring along the pencils and note paper. Maybe we should have a calendar to help us keep track of the days."

"No problem. I'll give one to John, and he can bring it along with the pencils and paper."

Rocky dropped Indian off at the Waldorf and then drove home and met with Colonel Carson and asked him to have John Smith come to meet him, so he could give him some supplies to take to the stakeout and a calendar, and he put all the items in a paper bag for John to take to their apartment. John soon came to Rocky's office and picked up the items. Rocky gave him the address of the apartment and information on where he could come into the apartment house from the alley.

John told Rocky he knew the area very well since he once lived only a couple of blocks away from that house when he was a kid growing up.

John also told him he would be sure the other two men assigned to working on the stakeout could find the apartment.

The next morning, Indian was at the rear of 208 Central Park Avenue at six forty-five, and only a few minutes passed before he was joined by John Smith.

John said, "Good morning, sir. I'm John Smith, and I'm here to help you on the stakeout."

Indian put out his right hand and said, "How do you do, John? I'm Indian Leader. Very glad to meet you and welcome to our little party."

John replied, "Yes, sir, I know who you are and I'm happy to join your party."

"Thank you. Shall we go up to our lookout position?" "Yes, sir, I'm ready to go."

Indian led the way upstairs and to their apartment at the front of the house. When they arrived at the apartment, Indian opened the door, and the two of them went inside the apartment.

John said, "Well, this is certainly nicer than most of the places we've worked on stakeout in the past."

"I think we were lucky to find this apartment directly across the street from the house we will be watching, and as a bonus, we can see right inside the house through their front window."

John said, "That's very good, Mr. Leader."

Indian replied, "Just call me Indian. We're going to be here for at least a couple of weeks working together, we need to become friends."

"No problem, Indian. I'm good with that."

John took out the items Rocky had sent with him and then John brought out two sets of field glasses.

Indian asked, "What do you have there, John?"

"Colonel Carson calls them field glasses. He used some like these when he was in the army. They let you see things that are far away from you. He said they make them in Germany. Indian, just take a pair of them and put the eyepieces up to your eyes and look through the window at the house across the street."

Indian took one of the pair of field glasses and put them up to his eyes and looked in the direction of the window across the street and said, "I can't see anything. It's just blurry."

John said, "You have to adjust them by turning the little rings that are by the eyepieces you are looking through."

Indian took the field glasses down from his eyes and saw the adjustment rings John told him about.

Indian turned the rings, and John said, "Indian, you need to hold the glasses up to your eyes, then turn the rings until what you are looking at becomes clear."

Indian put the field glasses up to his eyes and slowly began turning the rings until he could clearly see a book through the window and he said, "John, these are wonderful. I can see everything in the room like I was sitting right there. Please thank Colonel Carson for thinking of them to help us with our stakeout. They're great."

"I'll be sure to tell him. I'm glad you think they will help us." "I certainly do."

So began their stakeout of 208 Central Park Avenue, and for three shifts a day, they recorded the information of all the people who went in and came out of the house. They continued their stakeout for two complete weeks, and Indian and Rocky felt they had enough information to know when they should hit the people in the house.

They found on Friday, just before noon, all of what Indian called the Mafia lieutenants gathered at the house to report how things went for the prior week, and each of them brought in a large bag, which Indian and Rocky decided was the money each of the seven lieutenants' areas made for the week.

They went through the same routine each week; each of these men arrived prior to twelve o'clock carrying one of the large black leather bags.

They each took their place at a large dining room table set up in the front room, and at the head of the table was Don San Marco.

One by one, each gave a report of some kind to the group and to Don San Marco. The don would listen to each man's report of the week's activities, and they got so they could tell if Don San Marco was happy with the man's weekly report.

If he was happy, he would smile and say something that would make the man giving the report smile. However, if he didn't like the report the man gave, he would make a much longer reply, and the man giving the report would soon be frowning.

Many more of them were frowning than smiling after the reports were given. After the reports were finished, the men would always stay to have lunch of spaghetti and meatballs and some type of bread with Don San Marco.

Indian and Rocky decided after they finished their watches on Monday, they would hit the Mafia gang the following Friday. Rocky told Colonel Carson on Tuesday that they were finished with their stakeout, and his men could be assigned back to their normal duties. Rocky said, "Colonel Carson, Indian and I wanted to thank you and your people for their help in making the stakeout a success. We now have all the information we need, so we really appreciate all the work your people did for us."

23

INDIAN'S PAYBACK

Indian, Rocky, and Sean met on Thursday afternoon; and Indian explained in detail how he expected his plan to work out.

Indian said, "I want to keep Don San Marco alive if we can, because I plan to send him back to his grandfather with a message. I know that Rocky and I recognized the man who bumped into me on the stairway leaving the building after he killed Larry Larson, and Rocky, when that same man jumped into the carriage, getting away from the scene of his crime. He's the man who serves the food at the weekly Friday meetings of the Mafia. I think he must be Don San Marco's bodyguard, cook, as well as his personal assassin for anybody who the don wants bumped off. We need to get him in the kitchen before we go after the rest of the gang gathered around the table.

I'd guess he's the real killer of this bunch, which doesn't mean the rest of these Mafia men are pussycats. I'm sure they are all packing weapons.

"Sean, when we get to the house, you go into the back door that goes into the hallway, then guard the front door and the door into the apartment.

Shoot anyone who comes out of the apartment door or tries to open the door. Rocky's father-in-law has provided us with shotguns and plenty of ammunition. That's what we will be using to take these guys out. Rocky, do you have anything to add?"

"No, let's get these guys, but don't take any chances. We don't want to miss any of them. If we can't keep Don San Marco alive, it'll be too bad, but we don't want him to get away either."

Sean asked, "When the shooting starts, do you want me to come in?"

Indian replied, "No, you just make sure no one makes it out of your door. With two of us shooting shotguns, there's too big a chance you'd get hit or we might not take a shot for fear of hitting you. So whatever you do, don't stand directly behind the door. Got it, Sean?"

"Yes, sir. I've got it."

Friday morning, they met at the apartment at eleven o'clock and started watching the house to see if things were happening like they did the last two Fridays. Around eleven-thirty, the Mafia men began arriving at the house.

The three of them waited a little while, then Rocky said, "It's fifteen minutes to twelve, let's go."

The three of them went down to Rocky's carriage, and Rocky drove them over to the alley behind 208 Central Park Avenue. He pulled the carriage into the back of the house and tied the horses to an iron hitching post. They pulled the shotguns out of their bags and each grabbed several shotgun shells and loaded the shotguns with as many shells as they would hold. Then they put additional shells in their pockets. Both Indian and Rocky were wearing their six-shooters as well as having their shotguns.

Indian said, "Sean, we'll wait a few minutes so you can get in place before we go in, and we'll have to take care of the men working in the kitchen before we go into the dining room and start shooting. Just be ready for anyone trying to get out the door after we start shooting."

"OK, Indian. I'll be ready."

Sean went to the back door of the hallway and into the house. After Sean went inside the hall door, Indian and Rocky waited maybe a minute and opened the door to the kitchen. Indian saw the man who had bumped into him working at the stove, stirring spaghetti, and another man washing dishes at the sink. Indian motioned to Rocky to take the guy at the sink.

Rocky walked over and hit the man in the back of the head, and he slumped over the sink. At the same time, Indian had taken out his long skinning knife and slit the throat of the man who had killed Larry Larson.

This man still turned around to face Indian, and Indian put his knife directly into his heart. The man coughed once and fell to the floor. Indian slowly laid him to the floor.

Indian whispered to Rocky, "OK, you take the men on your left, and I'll take the ones on my right."

Rocky opened the door, and the men at the table all turned to look at who they thought would be bringing their lunch, only to see shotguns going off at them. As Rocky began firing, the men began falling on the floor. The man at the end of the table stood up and pulled his gun just as Rocky fired a shot hitting him in the face; his hands went up to his face, and Rocky fired another blast at his chest, and down he went.

At the same time, Indian was shooting the men on the right side, and they were falling one by one. Indian ran toward Don San Marco as he was pulling out his gun, and Indian hit him in the face with the barrel of the shotgun. The don dropped his gun and started holding his face. Then, Indian jerked the don up and pulled him into the kitchen and hit him again in the head with the shotgun barrel. The don slumped over, unconscious.

Then Indian went back into the dining room and began shooting each of the men he had shot with his shotgun in their head with his Colt 44.

Rocky was doing the same with the men he had shot.

Rocky yelled at Sean, "OK, Sean, we've got all of them. Come in here and help me carry these big black bags to the carriage."

"OK, Rocky."

Sean opened the apartment door and began gathering up the big black bags and started carrying the bags to the carriage.

Sean said, "Rocky, I'll take all the bags out to the carriage while you do whatever you need do here."

"OK, Sean."

After Indian finished making sure all the men were dead, he went back into the kitchen and took the don by his left arm and dragged him over to a meat-chopping block he found in the kitchen. There he took the son's left hand and placed it on the chopping block, pulled his trigger finger up on the chopping block, pushing his thumb and the other three fingers down to the side of the chopping block.

Indian picked up a meat cleaver from the chopping block, and with great care to be sure his aim with the cleaver was exactly where he wanted it to strike, wham! The cleaver went directly where Indian aimed and cut off the don's trigger finger on his left hand. Then, Indian let the left hand and arm fall to the don's side, took his right arm, and positioned his right hand and fingers exactly the same way as he did the left hand, and wham! Indian chopped off his right trigger finger.

While Indian was busy with the don, Rocky found a large pail of coal oil and a big stack of newspapers and began spreading the newspapers all over the floor and pouring coal oil on the newspapers. Indian pulled the don out of the kitchen and through the backyard to a small shed filled with trash cans.

Indian thought the don was exactly where he belonged, with the rest of the trash. Next, Indian took out a letter he had addressed to Don Giovanni, the head of the worldwide Mafia, which read:

Dear Don Giovanni,

This letter is sent to you as a warning to you, personally. I killed your son and could have killed your grandson, but I just cut off his trigger fingers, so he won't shoot any more of my friends or have them shot.

Keep your Mafia people away from the New York City Harbor Police Department officers. If you don't heed this warning, I will personally come to Sicily and kill you and your grandson and feed both of you to the pigs.

The Indian

After Indian put the note into the don's inside coat pocket, he saw Sean standing by the carriage after loading all the big black bags into the carriage.

Indian said, "I was just posting a letter to his grandfather."

Inside the house, Rocky had spread the newspapers and coal oil through all the downstairs rooms and in the central hallway. Then Rocky took a box of kitchen matches from the kitchen and began lighting rolled-up pieces of newspaper. Rocky began throwing the burning rolled- up newspaper in the central hallway, then into the living and dining room, and lastly, into the kitchen.

Rocky carefully locked and closed the back door and said to Indian and Sean, "Let's get out of here."

The three of them climbed onto the carriage, and Rocky calmly drove down the alleyway and took a left on Central Park Avenue. About the time they were maybe ten blocks away from 208 Central Park Avenue, they had to make way for a fire wagon traveling east toward from where they had just come. When the fire wagon arrived, they saw the house was in total flames, so all they could do was to keep the flames from spreading to the houses on each side of 208 Central Park Avenue. The firemen watched as the house collapsed into itself, when one of the firemen found Don San Marco and put bandages on his hands and asked a lady in the house next door if she would telephone for an ambulance. When the ambulance arrived, the don wasn't able to speak. He was still unconscious but breathing, so they took him to the hospital.

The following day, a newspaper story told about the fire and the man who was found outside the house. He was identified as Don San Marco, a Mafia member who was to be deported for overstaying his visa. When the immigrant officers took Don San Marco to the ship leaving for Italy, one of the officers handed Indian's letter that had been found on the don when he was taken to the hospital.

The officer said, "If I were you, I would be sure to give this letter to your grandfather. It looks like good advice."

When the doctors had asked him about his two fingers being cut off, he told them he had no idea. He didn't know anything about how the house caught fire or how he got in the shed by the trash cans.

The doctors said, "Sometimes, when things like this happen, the victim has no idea in his mind about what happened to him. The extreme stress to his brain blocks it all out."

The following day, Indian returned to the apartment he had rented and gathered up the few things they had left while a hack waited for him. Indian stopped by Lucy Brown's apartment and told her that he and his people had finished their work sooner than they expected, so the apartment was now empty.

Lucy said, "Let's see. I need to return a couple of weeks' rent to you for moving out before the month was over."

"No, ma'am, you don't need to do that. I've already charged it to our client and they were happy with our work, and we were happy with the apartment. It was exactly what we needed, but thank you anyway."

"Well, OK, Indian. You know you missed all the excitement around here yesterday. Did you see the house across the street burned down? I saw in the newspaper this morning some Mafia leader lived there. In this day and age, you never know who your neighbors are." "No, Lucy, I guess you don't. Thank you again for letting me rent the apartment, but my work here is done, and I'm heading home to Texas in a few days."

"Thank you, Indian. You are such a nice man. Good luck on your travels."

Indian's next stop was to meet with Rocky at his house. When Indian arrived, Rocky and Sean were waiting for him in Rocky's office.

Indian was quickly shown to Rocky's office, and when he walked inside, Rocky said, "Good morning, partner. How do you feel this morning?"

"Great, partner, couldn't be better."

Sean said, "That sounds good, so how is Robert doing now?" "I'm sorry to say, I haven't seen or talked to him for several days now. We seem to have been really busy."

Sean replied, "Yes, I guess you have been."

"Indian, Sean and I counted the money that was in those seven big black bags we took from the Mafia. There was over two hundred and fifty thousand dollars in them. What do you think we should do with the money?"

"Well, the one thing we can't do is to give it back to the people the Mafia took it from, which would be nice if it could happen, but it can't.

Since we can't give it back. I suggest we set up a fund for the widows and children of our fallen police officers. With that much money, you should have enough to buy all of them a home, so they never have to worry about paying rent."

Rocky said, "That's a great idea, but where are we going to tell people the money came from?"

Indian replied, "You just tell them a wealthy merchant donated the money to establish a fund to help the families of Harbor police officers who were killed in the line of duty because he appreciated the work the Harbor police were doing."

Sean said, "That's a great idea, and the fund should be named the Rocky Stone and Indian Leader Founder's Fund."

Indian answered, "I think it should just be called the Founder's Fund."

Rocky said, "I agree." Rocky added, "Indian, I just told Sean that as of tomorrow, I'm resigning, and he agreed to take over the chief's job. Now, I can get back to writing my dime novels. I've got a lot of new material for my stories from working with you two. That should be good for three or four new books."

24

GOODBYE TO NEW YORK

Indian went back to the Waldorf and told Serene, "I think it's time we go home, but I do want to see Robert and Joan off on their honeymoon in a few days before we leave. Robert has made arrangements to take Joan to London for their honeymoon, and he said while they were in England, he would be visiting with several of their suppliers and their customers."

Serene replied, "That sounds like you men: go on a honeymoon and all you're doing is thinking about business. How about thinking about romance, not business?"

"Well, I think he will be thinking a lot about romance while they are on their ship for several days and while staying in Europe for three months.

However, I've asked Robert to buy two registered Hereford bulls for us and make arrangements to ship them to Galveston for us."

"You did this without asking me what I thought about it." "Well, you've been talking about trying to improve the quality of our beef, and one of Robert's suppliers that I met while we were in New York told me about how much better the steaks were in England that were from Herefords than from our longhorns. I thought you would be thrilled that I was trying to help you develop a better quality steak."

Serene said, "Yes, I said all that, but you should have talked to me about it first. Besides, maybe my cows won't like an English lover."

"Serene, I guess we'll have to ask them."

"Yeah, I'll talk to them when we get home. I have some news for you from a visit I had with a friend of Latesha's."

"What kind of news? Is it good news?"

"Well, that may depend on how you feel about becoming a father."

"Serene, that's wonderful! I can't wait to tell my parents they're going to have a grandchild. When is our baby due?"

"Early in March."

"Wow, that's wonderful. I love you so much."

Indian put his arms around Serene and held her as close as he could and gave her the sweetest kiss she'd ever had.

Indian said, "We need to go see about Robert and tell him and Joan we're going home and that you're having a baby."

"OK, almost-a-daddy, let's go."

They walked over to the Sterlings' house, and Indian knocked on the door.

Claude answered the door and said, "Ms. Serene, welcome. Won't you and your husband come in?"

"Thank you, Claude. Will you tell Joan or Robert we are here?" "I will be happy to. However, they haven't come down yet this morning. Would you like to wait in the library?"

"Certainly, Claude, we will be happy to wait. I'll show Indian into the library if you would tell Joan we are here."

"Yes, Ms. Serene, please go into the library, and I will be happy to tell Ms. Joan you and your husband are here, waiting in the library."

Claude left them to go to tell Joan that Serene and Indian were waiting in the library.

Upstairs, Joan was saying, "Oh, Robert, we finally had our wedding night. I'm so glad you felt good enough for us to make love. It was wonderful, and can we do it again?"

"We sure can."

Joan rushed into Robert's arm, kissing him, and said, "I had no idea I would feel this good after doing it."

Then Claude knocked on their bedroom door, and she heard Claude say, "Ms. Joan, Ms. Serene and her husband are waiting for you in the library."

Joan replied, "Thank you, Claude. Please tell her we'll be down in a few minutes."

"Yes, Ms. Joan."

Joan said, "Sometimes your friends have very bad timing, and this is one of them."

Robert replied, "Joan, we will have many more honeymoon nights together."

"Promise, Robert?" "With all my heart."

Joan and Robert got dressed as soon as they could, and by the time they got down to the library, they not only found Indian and Serene, but Rocky and Latesha were waiting for them too.

Joan said, "I didn't get the notice of a meeting. Sorry we're late." Serene said, "Well, we just came to see how Robert was doing, and Latesha and Rocky had the same idea." Indian said, "So how are you doing, Robert?"

"I'm doing great. My wound is almost completely healed up, and I've got full use of my arm and shoulder."

Robert flexed his arm to show them, and Rocky said, "It looks like you've come a long ways since the last time we saw you."

"Yeah, the doctor gave me full release to do anything I want to do with my arm and shoulder now."

Indian said, "That's really great news, Robert."

Robert said, "It is great news. Joan and I are leaving for London next Friday on our honeymoon. We plan to be in Europe for four months, and I'm going to be doing some business while we are there."

Indian replied, "Robert, we're really happy for both of you. However, Serene and I have some news too. Serene's going to have a baby next March, so what do you all think about that?"

Indian heard Rocky say, "That's wonderful, Indian."

Latesha said, "It is wonderful news, and it's not the way I planned to tell you, Rocky, but here goes. Serene's not the only one that's going to have a baby, so are we, Rocky."

Rocky said, "Wow, are you kidding me?"

Indian said, "Poor choice of words, Rocky. Yes, I think she's got a kid in her."

Rocky reached for Latesha and held her and said, "No matter how you told me, it's wonderful news."

Indian said, "Congratulations, Rocky and Latesha. When did you two find out you were going to have babies?"

Serene said, "I asked Latesha if she could make an appointment for me with her doctor, and he told me I was having a baby. Then he checked Latesha over while we were at the doctor's office and found she was pregnant too."

Robert said, "Joan, we'd better get out of New York. There must be something in the water that's causing this condition."

Everyone laughed and agreed.

Serene said, "Boy, I can't believe all the changes that are going on in our lives."

Latesha said, "I don't think you have any idea of what new things will be coming in our lives in this new twentieth century if the people my father and I are working with succeed with their projects."

Robert asked, "Tell us, Latesha, about some of the things you think we're going to see."

"OK, I'll tell you some. My father is working with a man by the name of Ford out in Detroit who's working on a horseless carriage that can go anywhere in the country, even if you don't have good roads to travel on.

There are a couple of brothers out in Ohio who are working on a flying machine that doesn't use air to hold it up. You know my father works with Mr. Edison, and you never know what he may could up with next. He's working on a machine that can play music and another machine that can show moving pictures. Who knows how many other people may come along in the next few years with more ideas for new products to make our lives easier? I know my father has people searching for them all the time. He has a man that reads and studies every new patent that is issued every month, so he can decide if he thinks it might be a product that my father will be interested in investing in."

Indian said, "Wow, I can't believe all the new things we may see in our lifetime. Robert, you and Joan might want to wait a few years, and maybe you could fly across to London in one of those flying machines in eight or nine hours."

Everybody laughed, and Latesha said, "Just you wait, Indian. You may be traveling in one of those flying machine one of these days."

"Not likely, I've been flying through the air several times riding some of those broncos. I like staying with my feet firmly on the ground."

There was more laughter from all of them, including Indian.

Soon after that, the party broke up, and Indian said, "We will see you two off on your ocean voyage Friday before we go back home to Texas."

Rocky told them the same thing.

Friday came, and not only were Indian, Serene, Rocky, and Latesha there at the dock to see Robert and Joan off on their voyage, but Robert's parents, Tom and White Dove Smiley; Joan's parents, John and Patricia Sterling; along with their son, Michael; their adopted daughter, Shannon; and Joan's grandfather, Senator Wagner. They all wished Robert and Joan a safe and happy trip and to have a wonderful honeymoon with lots of love.

Finally, it was time for the two of them to board the ship; each of them were hugged and kissed by everyone who was there to see them off.

All of them watched as the ship slowly left the pier and began to head out to sea. When each of them could no longer see the ship, they all made their way back to their home or their hotel.

On Saturday, Indian and Serene and Tom and White Dove said their goodbyes to their new friends. John told Tom and White Dove, they would always have a home in New York with them anytime they could visit New York.

Rocky said, "Indian, I have to tell you, I've had the opportunity to work with a lot of people in my life, but none have been as great to work with as you. I consider you one of the best friends I have ever had in my life."

Indian replied, "I understand exactly how you feel. I feel the same way about you."

The two of them hugged each other, and neither Serene nor Latesha had ever seen that much affection for another man by either of their husbands.

Tom and Patricia told Indian and Serene, "You two know you are always welcome to come and visit anytime you come to New York."

Serene said, "Yes, I still know where my room is at your home." She gave both of them a hug and a kiss and then gave one to Michael and Shannon and told them to mind their parents. Both of them laughed and said, "Yes, ma'am, we always do."

When the four of them were finally on the train, Indian said, "We're going to go home with you to see my folks living on the Cherokee Indian reservation before we go on home to Texas. I have to tell my folks they are going to have a grandbaby."

Tom said, "Your folks are going to be so happy to see you two and to know they are going to have a grandchild."

The four of them traveled to Chicago and then changed trains to Kansas City. From Kansas City, they took a third train from Kansas City to Muskogee, Indian Territory. When they arrived in Muskogee, they were met by four Cherokee men with two wagons to take them to the Cherokee Indian reservation, where Tom and White Dove lived, as did Indian's folks. It took them three days to travel from Muskogee to the Indian reservation.

When they arrived there, Indian and Serene were taken over to where Indian's folks lived.

When Indian's mother saw him, she began to cry, and Indian took her into his arms and said, "What's the matter, Mother?"

She said, "I didn't think I would ever see you again, and your pa is going to be so surprised 'cause he said after you married a white woman, we would never see you anymore, but here you are."

Serene went over to Indian's mother and began gently stroking her hair.

A few minutes passed as the three of them stood together, and Indian's pa came into the house and said, "They told me you were here, Indian, but I didn't believe it, but here you and your wife are. I know I've told your ma a hundred times we would never see you again after you were married, but here both of you are. Welcome home, son, we've missed you so much."

Indian reached out his hand to his pa, and his pa took his hand and held it to his face.

After a little time passed, the four of them stood apart, and his mother asked, "Are you hungry, Indian? Of course you are, you're always hungry."

Indian said, "Wait a minute, Ma, we have something to tell you.

Why don't you tell them, Serene?"

Indian's folks turned their attention to Serene, and she said, "Ma and Pa, you're going to be grandparents. I'm going to have a baby in March."

Ma asked, "You are having Indian's baby?" "Of course, it's his baby." Pa asked, "When did you say the baby was coming?" "In March." Ma said, "That's good. It won't be too hot then, better time to have a baby than in summertime."

Indian said, "Pa, Ma, please come to live with us in Texas so our baby will have some grandparents because Serene's parents have gone to the other side."

Ma said, "You poor girl, you lost both your pa and ma?"

"Yes, my mother died when I was a very little girl, and my father was killed by rustlers, just before I met Indian."

Pa said, "You have no other family?" "No, no one, just Indian."

Ma said, "You do now. We'll come to live with you, won't we, Pa?"

"Yes, Ma, it's not good to not have a family or a tribe." Serene said, "Ma and Pa, you will be my family."

Indian said, "Now that's settled, I'm hungry." Ma said, "That's my boy."

Ma began working to fix them some food, with Serene trying to help without getting in the way. Indian and his pa began talking about the boys Indian grew up with, and Indian told his pa about Robert's wedding and that they had left on a really big boat going to a place called England.

The next day, the four of them left in two wagons to go back to Muskogee to take the train back to Kansas City in order for them to get the train back to San Antonio, where their wagon and team of horses were.

Indian's ma had never been off the reservation, and his pa had gone only as far west in Indian Territory where he found Indian when he was a small child.

Neither one of them had ever seen a train, so of course, they had never ridden in one. This trip was truly going to be an adventure for them.

Indian thought that he and Serene had never been parents before either, so let the adventures begin. His parents did fine after the first few miles riding on the train. They couldn't understand how the train always had a rail in front of it to go on. When they got to Kansas City, they saw buildings taller than any trees they had ever seen.

Pa asked, "What do all these people do in such big houses?"

Indian tried to explain to his folks, the people lived in these tall buildings and they had just a few rooms in the building, called apartments, and that many families lived in the building. They couldn't understand that some people lived on top of other people. Indian tried to explain that the buildings had many floors inside the building, but he couldn't make them understand the idea of floors. After two hours, they boarded the train to San Antonio and were soon leaving the Kansas City area. The next night, they arrived in San Antonio, and they stayed the night in the same hotel Indian and Serene had stayed in when they left San Antonio. Their hotel rooms were on the second floor, and they had to walk up the stairs to their rooms, and now his folks understood the idea of floors. They could see stairs going up to two more floors above them. They had never before in their life had such a soft bed, and they loved it.

Indian had to explain to them about the bathroom; they did use the ones on the train and in the train station in Kansas City but couldn't understand the one in the bedroom was only for their use and they didn't have to share it with anyone else.

The next morning, Indian got his wagon and his team of horses from the livery stable, and they started traveling to the Star Ranch. Two days later, they arrived at the entrance to the Star Ranch, and it took them another two hours of driving before they got to the ranch house. Pa and Ma looked at the big house that Indian and Serene lived in and saw the other buildings at the ranch headquarters, and Pa asked Serene, "Is all this yours?"

"Yes, it is, Pa. My pa spent fifty years building this ranch up for me to have it when he went to the other side."

"He sure must have worked very hard to give you someplace like this."

"He did. He worked very hard for all these years, just so I would have it one day."

Serene took Ma and Pa into the house and showed them their bedroom, which had its own bathroom, including a large bathtub and shower. She had to take a long time to explain how you could take a bath or a shower and wash your whole body at one time. Serene could see it was going to take some time before they would consider using a bathtub, but maybe the shower. Then she showed Ma her kitchen with its large stove and an oven to bake bread and things in. She introduced her to Ma Hayes, her cook and very close friend.

Ma Hayes and Indian's ma, Moonlight, seemed to connect as soon as they met; and Serene said, "Ma Hayes, I have something to tell you. I'm going to have a baby next March, and Indian's ma and pa have come to live with us to help raise our baby."

Ma Hayes said, "I think it's wonderful that you're going to have some family with you."

Serene said, "You are part of my family too." "Thank you, my dear."

The next day, Indian saddled up two horses, and Indian and Pa took a ride around the ranch so Indian could show Pa some of their cattle. Pa had never seen so many cattle in one place, and they were all owned by his son and daughter-in-law.

Indian said, "Pa, this is just some of our cattle. We have many more cattle scattered around the ranch."

"All these cattle are on your own land?" "Yes, they are all on our property."

"Well, son, maybe we could have steak for dinner sometime." "Pa, you can have steak anytime you want one."

"OK, how about tonight?" "You can plan on it, Pa."

That night, they had a big steak dinner for Pa and all the ranch hands.

Indian introduced his pa, Charlie Whitebird, and his ma, Moonlight, to all of them; and Serene made her announcement about her having a baby in March.

The winter passed by quickly, and it was soon March, and with Ma and Ma Hayes's help, Serene had her baby, a baby boy. Indian rode to Cuero, Texas, the next day to send a telegram to Rocky and Latesha about their son being born the day before and they had named him John Paul Leader.

The telegrapher operator said, "Congratulations to you and your wife, and thanks for coming into town today. You saved me from having to have my man ride all the way out to your ranch to deliver these two telegrams to you."

Indian opened up the first one and read it. It was from Rocky, and it said Latesha had her baby the day before, and they had a baby girl and named her Serene Joan Stone.

Indian said out loud, "I'll be damned."

The telegrapher operator asked, "Is there something wrong, Mr. Leader?"

"No, Sam, it's just that our friends in New York had a baby girl on the same day our son was born."

The second telegram was from Robert, and it said he and Joan were having a baby in November.

Indian said, "This telegram said that our other friends in New York are going to have a baby in November. I wonder what they will have."

Sam said, "Well, it will be one or the other." "Yeah, I reckon it will be."

Indian bought a box of cigars to take back to all his cowhands to celebrate the birth of their son. Indian climbed up in the saddle and rode home as quickly as he could so he could tell Serene all the news. Time passed by quickly that summer, and it was coming up to November very soon. One bright late October day, the man who delivered telegrams arrived at the Star Ranch and handed Indian a telegram. Indian took the unopened telegram inside the house to read it to Serene who was rocking John at the time. Indian opened the telegram and read it out loud so Serene and Ma and Pa could hear what the telegram had to say.

Indian read, "Joan had her babies today, one boy and one girl. All are doing fine. The boy's name is Tom Robert Smiley, and our girl is Joan Serene Smiley."

Indian then said, "Would you believe it they got two babies at a time? That Robert always wants to outdo me."

Pa said, "Reckon you two will have to get busy to get caught up with them."

Serene replied, "Pa, I don't think it's a contest. One at a time is good enough for me."

Indian said, "Pa, I think it's caused by that New York City water." Pa replied, "Son, I don't think that's what causes babies."

Ma said, "Pa, maybe we should go to New York and try the water." Pa replied, "No, Ma. I'm too old to go that far."

John started crying, and Serene said, "Like I said, one at a time is enough for me."

Indian took John from Serene and started carrying him around, and after some time, John went to sleep. Indian and Serene took John into his crib, and Indian slowly laid him down on his crib, but as soon as John was on his crib, he started crying again. Serene picked him back up and went back to her rocker and began rocking him again.

Serene said, "Like I said before, one at a time is enough for me."

THE END

ABOUT THE AUTHOR

Clark Selby was born in 1936 in Miami, Oklahoma, and attended school in Kansas and Oklahoma. He and his wife, Karen Serene Selby, live in Springfield, Missouri. He spent over forty-five years in the parking industry. Clark's work in the parking industry took him to over sixty countries on six continents.

During his years in the parking industry he served as Director of Parking, City of Hutchinson, Kansas; Assistant Director of Transportation and Parking, University of Iowa; Parking Consultant, De Leuw Cather & Company; Project Manager for a parking study in Perth, Western Australia.

He worked several years for Duncan Industries, as Sales and Service Engineer; Director of Manufacturing; Vice President and as President, then as President of Worldwide Parking. He retired to care for his first wife, Patricia after she became paralyzed and cared for her until she passed away.

Clark served in the Kansas Army and Air Force National Guard for six years and was a Sergeant in communications.

Clark and his wife, Karen travel as much as possible; they just completed an around the world cruise to six continents and twenty five countries. Clark loves writing novel, he always hopes his books tell a good story.

Two Cowboys in New York is the story of what happens when two cowboys come for a friend's wedding in the big city and find that the bride's father has disappeared. They offer to try to find out what happened to him after he left a meeting at the Port of New York, and they become entangled with the New York's Mafia who was robbing passengers at the port.

The Mafia never before in their history ran into adversaries like these two cowboys. Indian Leader and Rocky Stone just don't play by the same rules that the Mafia was used to facing.

Can Indian and Rocky find the bride's father and let their friend's wedding finally happen and corral the Mafia at the same time?

Clark Selby was born in 1936 in Miami, Oklahoma. Miami was the first town organized under the US Congress in Indian Territory in 1891. Today, it is the headquarters for six American Indian tribes.

He began writing novels after becoming the full-time caregiver for his first wife, Patricia, after she became paralyzed. He continued caring for her until she passed away.

The following books, which Clark authored, have been awarded the Cold Seal for Literary Excellence after reviews by the US Review of Books: Indian Leader Trail Boss, Together Forever, Dangerous Journey, The Power of Love, and Where's My Wife?

Clark and his wife, Karen, now live in Springfield, Missouri.